TWISTED SCARBOROUGH

J.B.Forsyth

For Sarah and the boys

Acknowledgments

A special thanks to Lindi for your invaluable input

And to Judithine for the cover art

Contents

Perigean Tide

I woke to the low beeping of the alarm and silenced it before it disturbed Laura. The room was awash with pale light and the digital display read 04:30. I dressed in the clothes I'd set out the previous night and went to Joel's room, giving him a shake which only made him wrap tighter in his blankets.

'Come on son. Gotta get up or we'll miss low tide.'

His eyes flicked open. 'The perigrin one?'

'Perigean,' I corrected with a smile. 'I'll get us some cereal, then we can get going.'

Ten minutes later we were in the car heading for South Cliff, driving through empty streets with the sky brightening in the east. We arrived at a deserted car park and drew up. I popped the boot for Joel to grab his fishing net and bucket, then we headed over to the cliff top. He was wearing red shorts, a yellow t-shirt and a green cap. An inverted traffic light with flapping sandals.

An item on yesterday's news had informed me that today was a perigean spring tide – an extreme change in the tides caused by an alignment of the sun and moon, when the moon is at its closest to earth. I explained it to Joel using a basketball, an apple and a marble, but failed to pique his interest until I mentioned all the new rock pools the low tide would expose.

I was hoping for a spectacle to impress Joel and I crossed to the cliff edge, never suspecting that I'd be so blown away by the sight that awaited us. To say the tide was way out would not be doing it any justice. The breaking waves had receded well beyond the outer harbour and the boats within were grounded and leaning to one side. The beach was twice as big as I'd ever seen it and the strip of sand closest to the sea seemed to have the consistency of mud – a surface you could imagine sinking in. Directly beneath us a familiar swathe of rock pools had grown, running out at least an extra fifty yards before disappearing into the waves. The seagulls were taking full advantage, a flock of hundreds picking over pools that had been safe from their probing beaks for who knows how many years. Banks of seaweed glistened in the strengthening sun and a gentle breeze lifted their redolence to where we were standing, a hundred feet above. An article I read in the paper said that despite the rare alignment of sun and moon, the difference between high and low tides would only be a few inches at most. But it seemed to be much more than that. I should have known then that something was wrong. And I should have turned around and taken Joel straight home.

Instead, we goggled at the view for a few minutes before Joel expressed what I was feeling. 'Wow!' He stuck a freckled arm out and pointed, a deeper level of wonder igniting his face. 'Look Daddy, there's a pirate ship.'

I squinted to follow the line of his finger, soon picking out the mast and prow of a boat, jutting above the waves. A prize the sea was unwilling to relinquish – even for a perigean tide.

'What did I tell you? Let's get down there before the tide comes in and covers it again.' It was my turn to point now. 'See that big flat rock,' I said, picking out the furthest one you could reach without getting wet. 'Let's get a picture of you on top.'

'Yeeaah! And I'll take one looking back at you.'

'You're on. Let's go.'

We practically ran down the chalkstone path, so keen were we to set foot on all that freshly exposed rock. I can't remember seeing another soul on the entire beach and it seems odd now that this didn't strike me as improbable. It was the middle of summer and the perigean tide had been widely publicised.

When we reached the rocky scar at the foot of the cliffs, I took the bucket and fishing net from Joel, fearing he might slip on the slimy rocks. We crossed treacherous patches of bladderwrack and oarweed and after a group of seagulls flew at him, I angled over and insisted we proceed with linked arms. Progress was slow and by the time we reached the flat rock we had both slipped several times and my boots were soaked through to my socks.

I climbed the rock, pulled Joel up after me and as low waves broke gently around its base, we marvelled at the scenery. We were within fifty yards of the sunken ship and for a time we watched the breakers roll around its mast and prow.

'Whose boat do you think it was?' I asked.

'A pirate with a big black beard and two wooden legs.'

In a trough of waves, we glimpsed a letter T etched into the boat's timbers: the first letter of its name.

'What do you think it's called?'

'Treasure Hunter,' he said in a flash and I smiled.

'Okay, let's do the photo, then we can go looking for a giant crab.'

'Giant crab?'

'The further the rock pool, the bigger the crabs. The ones out here will be real monsters.'

He looked around at the glistening pools with sudden anxiety and I realised I'd gone too far. This was supposed to be fun.

'I'm only joking,' I said, then held my hands out about ten inches apart. 'That's as big as they get. Whoppers, but not monsters.'

I left him on the rock and picked my way back several yards before pulling out my phone to take the photo, making sure to get the sunken ship in the picture. Joel chose to pose with his arms outstretched and his little hands scrunched into fists. I went back to help him down, but when I reached up, he was staring over my head, transfixed.

I turned and saw what he was looking at right away. Our position on the rocks gave us a view of the cliffs that beachcombers and sailors rarely got to see. Hidden behind a jut of cliff around which you wouldn't normally be able to walk was an arched opening that looked like it had been cut into the rock, rather than formed by natural processes.

'Can we look inside Daddy? It might be where the pirate hid his treasure. And when the sea comes in, it'll be all covered up again.'

'I tell you what. We'll go over for a closer look, but I'm not sure about going in. These cliffs can be dangerous.'

We stumbled over, stopping a dozen feet from the entrance to study a line of strange symbols engraved into the rock above the opening.

Joel knotted his brow. 'What does it say Daddy? I've never seen letters like that before.'

'That's because they're not letters son – or at least not any I understand.'

The sun was right behind us and as we moved closer our shadows leapt over the threshold. The walls inside were smooth and the floor covered with a grit of wet sand. On an empty beach with the sun on my back, my chest fluttered with the thrill of discovery. I've lived in Scarborough all my life and having never heard mention of any such tunnel, I felt sure we were the first to see it in a long time.

'Let's go in, before it fills with water,' Joel said, tugging my arm. I wasn't sure if the tide had turned, but the water was lapping hungrily at the entrance.

I looked at the cliff above the tunnel, assessing its stability with a layman's eye. I remembered reading something about freeze-thaw cycles bringing cliffs down, but the rock above the tunnel looked solid.

4

Nothing like the crumbly cliffs further south where houses were falling into the sea.

'I tell you what. You wait here while I check it out. And if it looks safe, I'll call you in.'

'Alright,' he agreed.

I left Joel at the entrance and went in hunched over, expecting the tunnel to collapse at any second. I took my phone out, thinking I'd need the flashlight app, but slid it back into my pocket when I realised the low light of the sun was more than enough to illuminate the passage.

Caves along the coast are usually daubed with graffiti and littered with empty beer cans. But there were no signs of human visitation in this one – only a covering of seaweed and a rough studding of limpets and sea anemones. The tunnel ran back about thirty feet, ending on a set of steps that spiralled upwards into darkness.

'Where do they go to Daddy?' asked Joel, making me jump.

'I told you to wait till I called you!' I scolded. But only half-heartedly. The discovery of the stairway was such a delight, it was hard to be angry with him.

'Sorry Daddy. But where do they go?'

'I've no idea.'

I took my phone out again, turned the flashlight on and shone it upwards. The steps were covered with seaweed, but there was none of the rockfall I had expected.

'Right, I'm going up to look around the bend, but you've gotta promise to stay here.'

'Promise,' he said, in a tone that seemed sincere. With my phone held at arm's length I started up. After about a dozen steps and out of sight of the tunnel the stairway became free of seaweed – clean cut steps that continued round and round. At first I expected them to deliver me to another cave, possibly a place where the hidden cache of treasure I knew Joel had in mind might be located. But as I got further up, I began to suspect they were a short cut to the cliff top – a long forgotten smuggler's stairway that would terminate on a trapdoor covered in dirt and overgrown with nettles. The seconds slipped by and I went higher and higher, beginning to feel more and more nervous about the distance opening between me and Joel, and more and more puzzled that I hadn't reached the top. I ascended another complete spiral and stopped, trying to visualise the height of the cliff. No more than a hundred feet I guessed, but it seemed like I had gone up a lot further than that. I decided to take another fifty steps and if I hadn't found the top, to return to Joel. But fifty steps later the top was still nowhere in sight. That was when the first wave of disquiet flooded me – a sudden watery dread that something was wrong. I turned back and almost sprinted down the steps, crashing into Joel after going only twice around the spiral.

'I told you to wait! That's naughty!' I said, truly mad this time.

It was only when I shone the phone near his face that I realised he was crying. 'What's the matter? Are you alright?'

'You've been ages Daddy and the water started to come in. I called and called and when you didn't answer I got scared.'

'That's nonsense. I've only been a couple of minutes and if you'd called, I'd have heard you. You've got to do as you're told. These caves are dangerous.'

I grabbed his hand a little too roughly and led him back down the stairway, but after only a single spiral we came back to the steps with the seaweed on. To my horror, I discovered he was telling the truth. The sea had flooded the tunnel to three quarters its height and was now lapping at the sixth step. I crouched and looked out. There was about twelve inches of air between the top of the rolling waves and the roof of the tunnel and the sun was still glaring in.

'It was only up to the first step when I came for you,' he said.

'I don't understand, I was only gone a couple of minutes.' The water had risen six feet in the time I had been away. My mind flailed, trying to make sense of it. In the end, I latched onto the possibility that such a sudden change in sea level was a consequence of the perigean tide – something my superficial study hadn't unearthed. But another part of me was beginning to suspect other forces at play – something to do with the symbols above the entrance and the strange stairway that had no place within the cliffs.

'Where do they go?' asked Joel, looking up the dark spiral.

'Nowhere. I'll have to call the coastguard,' I said miserably, already imagining the embarrassment of a rescue and having our names plastered all over the Evening News. 'It'll be alright.' I opened the dial pad, punched 999 and was promptly informed there was no signal. I looked into Joel's glassy eyes and felt something drop in the pit of my stomach. 'There's no signal in here.'

'So, what shall we do?'

I crouched and looked along the pocket of remaining air at the top of the tunnel, wondering if I could carry him out and swim for the shore. I put my hand into the water up to the wrist and realised it was a bad idea. The water was cold – icy cold. Much colder than it had felt through my boots a few minutes earlier. If asked, Joel would proudly inform you he was a good swimmer and could even back up his claim by showing you the purple 25m badge sewn into his swimming jammers. But I was there the night he qualified for that badge. He had to push himself off the bottom several times and the pool needed refilling afterwards; so much water did he swallow between one end and the other. He had improved since then, but not enough for me to be comfortable with him swimming out of his depth in a cold North Sea.

'How about I swim out and get help?' I said, knowing how this was going to go down before the words were out. And sure enough, his bottom lip started to wobble and his eyes began welling up. 'Okay, never mind – it's probably a bad idea anyway.' I didn't go into why. I couldn't leave Joel alone in this dark cave for even a minute and if something happened to me as I swum out, no one would ever find him. A terrible image flashed into my head, of Joel's fleshless bones laid out on the steps, still wearing his traffic-light outfit and floppy sandals.

I sat down and scrunched my hair. 'We get two tides a day about twelve hours apart. We'll just have to wait for low tide to come around again,' I said, already thinking about how worried Laura would be by then and how furious she would be when she found out what we'd been up to.

Joel sat down beside me, seemingly resigned to wait. But he was only seven and couldn't possibly understand how long twelve hours would take to pass in this damp cave.

'What shall we do while we're waiting?' he asked.

'I don't know, but I want to try something first. If I keep the light on the phone's battery'll run down. I'm gonna turn it off to see if we can get by without it.' In the ensuing darkness, Joel gripped my arm. 'It's okay, just wait for your eyes to adjust.'

It wasn't as bad as I expected. The sun was shining over the water onto our feet and we were able to see each other's faces well enough. But I knew things would be different when the tunnel filled with water as the seaweed went up another four steps.

'Right,' I said, trying to sound upbeat. 'If we're gonna be here for a while, we should at least make it fun. How about a game of Yesterday I Went to Market?'

'Okay,' he said and there was a distinct brightening of his voice. 'I'll go first – yesterday I went to market and bought a monkey.'

'Yesterday I went to market and bought a monkey and a submarine,' I said, hoping to get a laugh if he realised how useful a submarine would be right now. But he didn't. The game lasted all of about five minutes, by which time we had bought a monkey, a submarine, a jar of pickled onions (his favourite); a pair of arm bands (still no reaction), a PlayStation 4, a boat, a torch (which made *me* laugh); a pair of flippers, a hundred-and-ten-foot ice cream, a ham and mustard sandwich and a horse with a glass eye, before he finally gave up, not being able to remember the flippers.

'I'm thirsty,' he said, flopping against my shoulder. I usually took a bottle of water and a pack up when we visited the seaside, but I hadn't bothered that morning as I didn't expect to be out more than a couple of hours.

'Sorry Joel, but there's nothing to eat or drink until the tide goes out again. But when we get back, you can have anything you want. I promise. Even a hundred-and-ten-foot ice cream sprinkled with pickled onions.'

'Yuk,' he said, accepting our lack of provisions without moaning, again, most likely because he didn't understand how miserable twelve hours would be without food and water.

A terrible thought occurred to me as we stared into the water: if this morning was the lowest tide, would the next one be low enough for us to get out. I remembered reading that the heights of the tides drift slowly with the phases of the moon, but this perigean tide had surprised me already and I couldn't be certain of anything.

'I think we should try the stairs Joel.'

'But you said they didn't go anywhere.'

'We'll I'm not sure, because I never went all the way up. I didn't want to leave you alone for too long.'

'Can I come with you?'

The first time I went up I wanted him to stay at the bottom, but things were different now and I didn't want him out of my sight. 'Why not? You can count the steps with me. How high can you count?'

'Infinity and ten.'

I smiled, but as we began to climb, I felt a new wave of unease settle upon me. We went upwards, counting out loud and using only the dim light of my phone to see by, both of us puffing by the time we got to fifty. Joel announced the hundredth step with the triumph that infects all children when reaching this milestone; whether it's the number of

9

skips over a rope or the number of seconds holding their breath. But after another full spiral his excitement evaporated and when he counted the one-hundred-and-seventieth step, he flopped down without warning. 'Need a rest.'

I sat down without protest, wiping at the dew that was beading my hairline. 'How many more do you think there are Daddy? It's like we're going up magic steps that go on forever.'

In another place, I might have laughed and ruffled his hair, but back there on that dark stairway his words were truly spine tingling. What he said stirred the fear that was simmering in my gut and for a few seconds I couldn't speak. As I sat there holding Joel's sweaty hand, I thought about the steps that ran up the side of the Grand Hotel – steps I used to run up before he came along. I counted them once and there was one-hundred-and-fifty-two. Was it possible an even higher stairway could fit into the cliffs? Perhaps I thought – but only just.

'Are you ready Daddy?' asked Joel, recovering before I could. 'We've got to be close now.'

But we weren't.

Two hundred came and went, without the same degree of enthusiasm from him and by the time we got to three hundred, a liquid dread was seeping into my bones. The stairway was winding forever upwards without a single feature on its smooth walls to differentiate each spiral from the next. We stopped again puffing hard and I could hear a jittering in my voice when I spoke. 'I think we should go back down and wait for the tide.'

'Okay. I don't like these steps anymore Daddy, they're a bit scary.'

You're not kidding, I thought, but I told him they were just a set of silly old steps and that we'd be out of there in no time. I hugged him close and kissed him on the top of his head - the tips of his bent little knees shining eerily in the light of my phone. After the strange experience of my first descent, I didn't ask him to count the steps on the way back down, counting them in my head instead. And when a seaweed covered step appeared on the exact count of fifty, I almost screamed.

'Aw Daddy, you're hurting me?' said Joel. I realised I was squeezing his hand and relaxed my grip. 'It was much quicker coming down, wasn't it? ... Wasn't it?'

'Yes Joel, it was,' I said, trying to keep my voice level. I was coming apart inside, but I wasn't about to let my little boy see.

'I'm thirsty.'

'I know,' I snapped, 'but like I told you before - there's nothing we can do about it!' I felt instantly guilty and apologised. My mouth was as dry as a salt sachet and Joel had been working just as hard on the stairs. I bent to look along the top of the tunnel and was dismayed to find the water level hadn't changed a bit. And the sun was still in the same place, shining in through that same twelve-inch channel of air. I looked at my phone and checked the battery: half full. I warned Joel again and turned it off. 'We'll just have to wait.'

'Shall we play another game?'

'Maybe later. Let's rest a while for now. If you lie against me, you could try and get some sleep.'

'But I'm not tired.'

'Just rest then, while Daddy thinks.'

Joel curled up on my lap. He watched the water lapping at the steps for a few minutes then shut his eyes. He slept through what were easily the longest two hours of my life, but in all that time the water level never changed and the sun continued to shine over its surface. I could feel the nervous energy building inside me. By now Laura would have tried to ring and would be wondering where we were.

We waited and waited and when 6:00 pm showed on my phone, I realised something had to be done. 'I'll have to swim for it Joel.'

'No Daddy, you promised.'

'It's teatime and there'll be loads of people on the beach. All I need to do is swim out, call for help and swim back in. I'll only be a few minutes and I'll leave my phone.'

'But I'm scared.'

'Look son, the water level hasn't changed for hours. This might be the only way we're getting out.'

He looked frightened, but when he looked at the water again, he seemed to accept what needed to be done.

I stripped to my underwear and stepped down into the sea, gasping as I submerged my chest. I touched the bottom with the next step and discovered that if I stayed on tiptoes, I could keep my face above the waves.

'Just a few minutes and I'll be back.'

Joel laid on the lowest dry step to watch my progress. I inched away, bracing against the walls for stability.

'Is it cold Daddy?'

'Really cold, but I'll be alright,' I said, turning to face him so he could see I was okay. I went slowly, listening to my breath echoing along the roof of the tunnel. Eventually my probing hand found an outer edge and a few ballet steps later I was out under the arch and treading water in the North Sea. The current pulled me away and I was soon bobbing up and down among bigger waves, catching a glimpse of Joel's worried face only when my elevation was right. After a quick look at the cliff to mark the tunnel's location, I orientated myself onto a line that would take me around the jut of headland and broke into a steady front crawl, realising I was going to be much longer than the two minutes I'd promised. I stroked around the cliff with my head down and when I looked up there was nothing but miles and miles of water and sheer cliffs. Scarborough's South Bay was nowhere to be seen....

I woke up calling Joel's name. Laura moaned and reached over. 'You alright babe?'

'Yeah. Sorry. Just a bad dream that's all.' I threw back the blankets and let the air cool my moist skin, before pushing to my feet. I went straight to his room, needing to look at his sleeping face. But he wasn't in his bed. I flicked the light on and fell against the door frame. His bed was made – not with his Star Wars duvet and pillow slips, but with a plain red set. His dinosaur posters were gone – replaced by modern art prints, and his shelves, usually crammed with fossils and action figures, were supporting nothing more than Laura's college books and a couple of house plants. My whole body shaking, I staggered back to our bedroom and flicked the light on. 'Where's Joel Laura? Where's Joel?' She moaned and when she turned away, I stormed over and shook her. 'Where's Joel?'

She sat up, suddenly annoyed. 'What are you talking about?'

'Our son Joel! Where is he?'

She looked at me as if I'd lost my mind.

'We haven't got a son. It's just a bad dream.'

I can't tell you much of what happened afterwards, except to say that before noon there was a doctor in our house giving me drugs to keep me calm. He told me I was suffering acute psychosis brought on by an incredibly vivid dream, but even in my disturbed state, I could see he wasn't convinced. By the time he arrived, Laura was in tears and I was turning the place upside down trying to find evidence of Joel – emptying cupboards and clicking maniacally through picture and video files. In the end, I called my parents who denied all knowledge of their grandson and rushed to our house, so worried were they by what I was saying.

That day I scared my family with descriptions of a boy I claimed to be my son and stories of days they had spent in his company: Mum picking brambles with him on the old railway track; Dad taking him on a big red speedboat for his birthday and Laura and I building a driftwood fire with him on Cayton Bay, while we camped beneath the stars. Stories that rolled off my tongue with the easy recall of events that actually happened. But they all just stared at me and held their faces, Mum and Laura eventually bursting into tears.

Dreams fade, but Joel hasn't. How could he? Ask yourself, what would it take to convince you that the person you love most in the world doesn't exist? Or worse still, *never* existed? And it's not the same as grieving for one who's passed away, because I've no photos or hands-print paintings to cry over. No baby clothes, dinosaur set or Star Wars bedspread. No nothing. Joel was plucked from the universe and deleted from history – a cruel trick I'm now sure had something to do with those strange symbols above that tunnel.

I spent the better part of two years in a mental health hospital and only recently got out. Laura left me and I've moved back in with my parents. She said I'd invented Joel and she could no longer stand by while I grieved for a 'figment of my imagination'.

'*We* haven't lost a son!' she bawled before slamming the door, '*You* have!'

It was for the best though, as I couldn't bear to hear her talk that way when my favourite memories are of the three of us together.

Despite the doctor's attempts to expunge Joel from my head, I feel his presence now more than ever. As I type these words, I sense him behind my left shoulder and looking up, I can see his reflection in the window – standing there in his traffic-light beach clothes. And son... if you are reading these words, I love you so much. I think about you every day and I would give anything to be able turn around right now and give you a great big Daddy hug.

When I left hospital I spent the whole day down at the harbour, asking fishermen and divers if they had ever seen that tunnel. None had. Local history books make no mention of it and historians have never heard of it. The next big perigean spring tide will be in fifty years. I'll be eighty-one years old, but I'll be there at low tide, searching for that tunnel.

Books To Die For

Ricky slid a book from the shelf and studied the cover. It was a relatively new book and he held it to his nose, sniffing deeply as he zipped through the pages. Someone giggled and he turned to see a pretty girl smiling at him. She had long black hair, held back with a yellow band.

'I'm sorry,' she said, 'it's just I do the same sometimes. There's nothing like the smell of a book to get you in the mood for reading — although the ones in second-hand book shops are usually a bit musty.'

'It's VOCs that gives them that smell,' he said brightly. 'Volatile organic compounds that make up the paper and adhesive and get released over time. If they've been exposed to smoke or damaged by water, they release those smells too... This one's got a new smell though.' He felt himself flush, suddenly embarrassed by his science talk. But she didn't seem to mind.

'Really,' she said, eyes lighting up with genuine interest. 'VOCs. I'll have to remember that. What you got there anyway?'

'This,' he said, turning the book in his hand. 'I don't really know. The title just grabbed me: *Absence*. And the cover's a bit different.' He raised the book to show her the girl on the front. She was standing in a field, leaning heavily on a crutch. 'Far too many fantasy books have swords, dragons and hooded magicians on the cover.'

'True,' she laughed.

'You read fantasy?'

'Yeah, mostly actually. But I still like a bit of girly stuff.' Now *she* seemed suddenly embarrassed, turning away to ease the book she was holding back into the bookcase. He looked up and saw the sign above the section: ROMANCE. He got a whiff of her perfume as she turned back and flicked her hair - like fresh flowers tossed in a breeze.

'What do you think of the way he arranges the books?' she asked, breaking an awkward silence. 'A bit quirky don't you think?' He looked at the shelves and saw something he hadn't noticed before. On every other shelf the titles of the books read from bottom to top instead of top to bottom. 'I asked him about it one day and he said it's because of the arthritis in his neck. It pains him to spend all day tipping his head to the right. This way he can alternate sides.'

'I hadn't noticed. It's amazing what you don't see when you're focused on something else.' He thought about adding something sciency on inattentional blindness, but managed to restrain himself.

'Take one out that's been put in the other way – they're all upside down.'

He eased one out and had to turn it top to bottom to read the blurb. 'Yeah, that is odd.'

'Well, I'd best be going. It was nice talking to you.'

'You too.'

She brushed past him, trailing tantalising notes of her flowery perfume. But before she disappeared from the aisle he called after her. 'Hey! Do you fancy going for a drink sometime?' His face was suddenly aglow, his heart racing at his unaccustomed boldness.

She turned full to face him and for several excruciating seconds, appraised him with amused eyes. 'Alright. Why not?'

A week later he was waiting for her outside the bank. She was eighteen minutes late, though he wasn't entirely sure. He had been so embarrassed making the date that it was quite possible he'd misremembered the time. And on top of that, he hadn't taken her phone number or asked her name. His heart fluttered several times in false alarm, when a pretty face appeared in the flowing crowd, but when 2.30 came and went he was sure she'd stood him up. Or worse -

that the girl was watching from some nearby window, laughing at him with her friends. He walked away, cursing himself for believing someone like her would be interested in a nerdy guy like him.

He decided not to waste his visit to town and to pay a visit to Books To Die For. There was a slim chance the girl would be there, but to be in the very place she had arranged a date at the time when she was supposed to be on it, required a degree of audacity he didn't think her capable of. But despite this reasoning he did a complete scour of the shop before relaxing into his browsing. There was only one other customer in – a tall man with a grey beard and little specs who was currently bent over, pulling out books in rapid succession. When Ricky tried to pass, he straightened with the air of a headmaster greeting a wandering pupil. 'Did you know this building is over three hundred years old?'

'No. I didn't.'

'It was once home to Dick Turpin and it was partially destroyed by German gunboats in World War One.' Ricky looked around as if expecting to see cracks in the walls. 'Fascinating eh?' The man pulled out another book and looked at the cover with a pleasurable exclamation. 'Ah! This'll do me,' he said with a smile. 'Good speaking with you.'

When he disappeared around the corner Ricky continued to the SCIENCE FICTION section where he found a young man of about his own age standing in the aisle. He was moving his hand from side to side as if showing his large wristwatch to a row of books. He stepped in to allow Ricky to pass, then continued the strange movement. He pulled a book out every now and again, added it to a pile on the floor before typing something into his watch and repeating the process. Ricky watched from the corner of his eye, fascinated. And when his curiosity finally got the better of him, he asked what he was doing.

'This,' the man said, seemingly delighted by the question, 'is a new smart watch and it's proper sick. I just type what I'm looking for, scan

17

it across the shelf and if it's there, it lights up and gives me a buzz. I could ask the shopkeeper, but this is way quicker.'

'Wow,' said Ricky, genuinely impressed. 'I wouldn't mind one of those. What else does it do?'

'Lots.' He took a random book from the shelf and held it to his watch. The display lit up and he began to read: '123,793 words and at my reading speed of 182 words per minute it would take me 11.33 hours to read it. This particular book has been on this shelf for 57 days and seven people have handled it.'

'Never. You're winding me up.'

'I'm not – look.' He angled the screen so Ricky could see. 'It uses remote motion sensing, fingerprint analysis and some other shit I don't understand... Hold your hands out and I'll show you.' Ricky did as asked, the young man scanned the watch over his fingers and walked away, scanning the shelves from top to bottom. Every so often he pulled a book a third of the way out and left it there. He reached the end of the aisle and returned with a satisfied smile. 'Take a look. You my friend, have handled every one of those books at some time or other.'

Ricky went down the aisle, checking the books and sliding them back in. And sure enough, he remembered looking at every one. 'That's fucking awesome. I'm definitely getting one of those.'

'You won't be sorry,' the man said, picking up his pile of books and starting away. 'Nice meeting you.'

After another ten minutes browsing, Ricky settled on a fantasy novel (no sword, dragons or hooded magicians on the cover) and took it to the counter where the shopkeeper was taking books from a sports bag and placing them in a pile on his desk. As Ricky approached, he raised one reverentially, holding it to the light and speaking to its cover. He was half turned away, but Ricky caught a little of what he said – something about it being away a long time and how it must be hungry. When the shopkeeper sensed him, he broke off mid-sentence and smiled, taking his selection from him and reading the pencil-marked price written on the inside. 'That'll be just two pounds,' he said and as Ricky dug into his pocket he twisted away and whispered to the book, turning back as if such behaviour was all part of a normal sale. 'Is there anything else I can help you with?'

'No, that's all thanks.' He handed the shopkeeper a five-pound note and he made change from a wooden money box. 'Keeping busy?'

'Ticking over. But I've been pulling my hair out today. Had someone in earlier looking for some Agatha Christie. I've got a sack load somewhere, but I've looked everywhere and can't find a single one.'

'That's mystery books for you.'

'That's right,' said the shopkeeper, as if there had never been a truer statement. 'They can be so vexing sometimes – disappearing in one place and reappearing in another. And who priced them up, I never could fathom.'

Ricky smiled, thinking the shopkeeper was pulling his leg, but it dropped away when he realised he was deadly serious.

'Someone was just telling me Dick Turpin once lived here.'

'Dick Turpin?' the shopkeeper replied with a puzzled frown.

'The man who just left told me. He also mentioned the damage the place took in World War One.'

The shopkeeper shook his head. 'I've been here thirty years and I've not heard anything like that. Besides, this place wasn't built until the 1930s … Where did he tell you this?'

Now it was Ricky's turn to frown. 'Where? Just there, on the first aisle.'

'Ah. General Fiction. Looks like *they're* not behaving either.'

'Oh,' said Ricky. The shopkeeper was obviously a tad eccentric. He took his change and was halfway out the door when he turned back. 'I don't suppose you've seen a girl about five ten with long black hair, held back with a yellow band. She was in here last week.'

There was a flash of something in the shopkeeper's eyes, but he shook his head. 'Sorry, I haven't seen anyone of that description.'

'You told her why you alternate the book spines,' said Ricky, hoping to prompt his memory.

'I don't recall such a conversation, but that's not to say I didn't have it. I talk to lots of people over the course of a week. Was she a friend of yours?'

'Not really. I got talking to her in here the other day and just wondered if she'd been in again. Not to worry though. Thanks anyway.'

When Ricky got home he searched the internet for new smart watches, but couldn't find any claiming to do the things he witnessed earlier. After an hour, he gave up in frustration, took his novel to the sofa and opened it up. Written in pencil on the inside cover was the price with the word FANTASY above it. He remembered now how the shopkeeper had dismissed his customer's Dick Turpin story as somehow related to the fact he had been standing in the GENERAL FICTION section. And how he blamed his MYSTERY books for going missing. He turned to chapter one, but stared through the page instead of reading. Whilst standing in the FANTASY section, he had hit it off with the type of girl he often fantasied about. And she had been standing in the ROMANCE SECTION. Then there was the young man with the seemingly improbable watch, who had been browsing the SCIENCE FICTION shelves. He smiled at the odd coincidences, turned to chapter one and started to read.

The next weekend Ricky was back at Books To Die For. He had nothing particular in mind so he browsed the shelves, waiting for something to jump out. He knew there was a chance of seeing the girl and was hoping to bump into her again. It would be a bit awkward, but as the week went by it had narked him more and more that she'd stood him up. That sort of thing had happened to him at college, but this was the first time in his adult life. He wasn't planning to cause a scene or anything. If they crossed paths, he would simply smile and say hello, in the hope that some genuine reason had kept her away. He was also hoping to see the young man with the cool smart watch, so he could ask him where he got it.

There were two other customers in the shop: a man in the HUMOUR section who was leaning against a pillar laughing to himself, and a woman on the next aisle who Ricky could partially see through a gap between books. She was looking up and down her aisle and, thinking no one was watching her, she tucked a couple of paperbacks into her shoulder bag and covered them with a scarf. It had never occurred to Ricky that anyone would steal from a second-hand shop. The books were cheap enough and had little resale value. She disappeared from view, reappearing briefly at the end of his aisle as she made her way to the front, three more books held against her hip. He followed her to a bookcase which gave him full view of the counter. It was obvious she wasn't going to declare the hidden paperbacks and his heart rate soared as thoughts of intervening began to take form.

He watched the shopkeeper give her a warm smile and start totting up, repeating his strange habit of whispering to each book before handing them back. He felt the moment for action arrive when her change was handed over, but he didn't move. In the end, he had no stomach for creating an ugly scene. If she was desperate enough to steal them, he figured her life would only be made worse by a prosecution. So, he watched her swish out through the door instead - the stolen goods swinging from her shoulder.

The shopkeeper came out from behind his counter, gave him a nod and walked past him into the racks. Ricky continued his aimless browse until he came to the shelf from which the woman had stolen the books and saw a row of Ian Rankin novels (upside down) leaning into the space she had taken them from. His eyes went up to the top of the bookcase and the word CRIME glared down at him from a white card. The woman had committed a crime whilst browsing the crime section – another curious example of an event linked to the genre of books that surrounded it.

He wandered back through the shop, studying the customers with new eyes. There were four customers in the shop now. The man in the HUMOUR section was still laughing to himself, but the other three were acting completely normal. There was a woman browsing the LOCAL HISTORY section, a man reaching for some top shelf PHILOSOPHY and a teenage girl, crouched in the SHORT STORY section.

He decided to get some air, but halfway along the rear aisle, he passed a door in the back wall that was usually closed and which he previously assumed led to the shopkeeper's residential areas. It was propped open with a wedge now and there was a sign above the door that read: HORROR.

A sign he'd never seen before.

The door hadn't been open on his first walk around the shop and he realised the shopkeeper must have just this minute opened it. Inside, a bare bulb of low wattage hung from the ceiling, casting a cone of weak light into a storeroom lined with bookshelves. His pumping heart told him it was the last place he wanted to go and he almost hurried away. But this was getting silly he told himself – he couldn't give in to visceral reactions based on superstitious thinking. What could possibly happen to him in the HORROR section of a second-hand book shop?

He stepped in and looked around. There were whole shelves of Stephen King (upside down) and whole shelves of Dean Koontz (right way up). But about chest height, going right around three walls were books that had been put in the wrong way altogether – spines hidden at the back and pages facing out. The page ends were yellow and grey and he was instantly reminded of the filter system in the mouths of baleen whales. He puzzled over this for a time. He could understand the whole upside-down thing, but couldn't see how this system helped anyone. It was then he got a whiff of perfume, the same flowery tones his date had been wearing. His heart leapt and he turned sharply, expecting to see her standing in the doorway. But she wasn't. He stepped out of the room and seeing no one on the back aisle, he went back in sniffing at the air. The smell was still there, but it was so faint he began to wonder if it was just his imagination.

He had no real interest in horror, but curiosity got the better of him and he reached for one of the books with the pages pointing out, interested to find out which authors the shopkeeper had chosen to treat this way. As his hand went forward his fingers slipped between the pages. His arm jerked back, but the pages tightened on him before he could escape, trapping him from his first knuckle down. He screamed as something began munching on his fingers. Glassy pain lanced up his forearm and blood began to ooze from the pages, sending a blossoming stain to either side.

'Help!' he screamed, bracing a hand and foot against the shelving and trying desperately to pull free.

The man from the HUMOUR section answered his call, stepping into the room with wide horrified eyes. But then his face broke into a broad smile and he began to laugh – so hard he ended up doubled over, clutching his chest and pointing at his trapped hand. Soon after the woman from the LOCAL HISTORY section arrived and looked in with something like curiosity. 'Fifty-five people have gone missing in Scarborough over the last 30 years,' she said. 'Just came into town and simply vanished. Some were last seen coming into this very shop. I wonder if this room had anything to do with it.'

'WHAT YER DOING!?' screamed Ricky. 'THERE'S SOMETHING IN THE BOOKS AND IT'S GOT MY FINGERS!'

A teenage girl, who through his writhing agony he recognised from the SHORT STORY section, appeared alongside her and began reading from the back of a book. 'Ricky meets a girl in a shop of magic books that have the power to tailor reality to suit their genre. After several uncanny experiences, he is drawn to the HORROR section with tragic results.' She shook her head and frowned. 'It's a bad blurb... Gives too much away.'

She stepped aside for the man who had been browsing the PHILOSOPHY section. 'Calm down Ricky. Epicurus tells us it's irrational to fear death: "If death causes you no pain when you're dead, it's foolish to allow the fear of it to cause you pain now." '

The customers crowded the entrance to the little room, looking at him with the solemn expressions of professional mourners. Tears of agony streamed Ricky's face, but through his pain he was still able to appreciate the horror of his situation.

'AAAAAAAH! GET ME THE FUCK OUT!'

The shopkeeper pushed to the front and looked in with satisfaction, the lenses of his spectacles reflecting the light of the dim bulb.

'Patience young man and watch your language. My books don't like profanity. It might help to think of the girl you were so anxious to find, as you'll soon be joining her on the other side. She paid us a visit this morning and had the honour of becoming breakfast... Some readers hunger for books, but these books are ravenous for readers.'

The man from the HUMOUR section had finished laughing, but the shopkeeper slapped him on the shoulder and he began again; eyes soon streaming tears which dripped off his chin.

Ricky thrashed hysterically, his right hand inadvertently penetrating the opposite bookcase; slipping through the pages and into the agonising gnash of more teeth. He screamed and threw his head back, becoming a writhing human crucifix. His head touched the turned-out pages of the rear bookcase and his hair slipped inside. They gripped and pulled him in like a mangle, lifting his scalp and drawing his head backwards. His fingers broke into splinters and his hands sunk into the pages up to the wrists. Wooden teeth went to work on his head and cracked his skull; the appetite behind them, sucking his leaking brains in through the pages.

'They say books are the food of the mind,' the shopkeeper said. 'But in my shop that food chain works in reverse.'

And with that he flicked the light off and kicked the wedge out from under the door. It swung into place with a gentle click, leaving Ricky alone in the munching darkness.

The Sandcastle Man

Toby's mum dropped the beach bags with a sigh. 'This'll do,' she said, pulling a towel out and spreading it on the sand. She took a baseball cap from a side pouch and pressed it onto his head, proceeding to cover him in green sun cream that smelt of apples.

'Can I have some crisps?' he asked as she worked it into his shins.

'If we eat everything, you'll be hungry later.'

'But I'm hungry *now*.'

She pointed to the clock tower on the pier. 'When the big hand points up, that'll be one o' clock. We'll picnic then. It's not long.'

Toby stared at the clock with a screwed-up face. The big hand was just passed the bottom and didn't seem to be moving at all. It was going to be ages before it reached the top. He was a six-year-old living in the here and now - the wait of a minute like that of an hour and that of an hour, like a million years.

'There you are, all done,' she said, kissing his forehead and wiping her hands on the towel. I'm going to sunbathe – but I want to be able to see you at all times. There's too many people here and if you go too far, it'll be like trying to pick you out of a Where's Wally book.'

Toby looked around and saw she was right. They were close to the lifeboat house and there were hundreds of people on the beach – all with deck chairs and towels; the sand between them littered with buckets, spades, frizbees and balls. Just like one of those books. There was more space further along the beach and he wished they'd gone there.

His mum settled on the towel and began rubbing herself with cream. 'Go for a paddle if you want, but go there and back in a straight line. If you lose sight of me, remember we're set up right in front of the fish and chip shop. See?'

Toby saw, and in doing so got a waft of fish and chips. They would be having a picnic soon, but he would have preferred to quieten his rumbling tummy with fish and chips, rather than scotch eggs and jam sandwiches. When she laid back, he padded to the sea and walked in. It was colder than he expected and he braved it only to his knees, entertaining himself by jumping the froth of dying waves. He soon noticed some older girls swimming further out and for a time he just stood in the lapping water, marvelling at their bravery.

When he turned to go back, he couldn't see his mum among the countless sun worshipers. He remembered what she'd said about the chip shop and sure enough she was on a line directly from it, propped on her elbows and waving; smiling under her floppy sun hat.

'Was it cold?' she asked when he returned with pink shins.

'Freezing.'

She rubbed his legs with a towel to warm them up, but all it seemed to do was scratch sand into his skin and he pulled away.

'Why don't you make sandcastles?' she suggested. 'And if we're still here when the tide comes in, we can watch them get swept away.'

This sparked his imagination and he took his bucket and spade to a vacant strip of beach by her feet. He filled the bucket with damp sand, scraped the top flat and flipped it over. Then after several pats on the top he lifted it free, leaving a sandcastle with most of its top missing. He looked into the bucket and frowned at the rest – stuck in the damp depressions that formed the turrets. It didn't upset him like it used to though. Last week he'd cried after producing a row of broken castles, but his mum pointed at Scarborough Castle and said all the best ones had bits missing. Or-fen-tic was how she described them.

He made three more sandcastles to form four corners of a square, then made another in the centre before sitting back to admire his work. A breeze picked up, carrying from the arcades a delicious ribbon of doughnut aroma. Another favourite and his little stomach stretched to what felt like cavernous proportions. He looked over at the clock. The big hand was halfway to the top and he hoped that by the time he put some finishing touches to his castles it would be time to eat. He leant forward to build some bridges between them and froze when he caught sight of a huge sandcastle a little further along the beach – one that looked like it belonged in a Disney film.

He stood to get a better view, but his line of sight was partially blocked by an old lady with a sun visor, who was reading a big newspaper. He opened his mouth to ask his mum if he could go for a closer look, but she was snoozing and he decided not to wake her. The sandcastle wasn't too far away and he only wanted a quick look. He bare-footed it across the sand, weaving through towels and parasols and when he arrived at the sandcastle he stood and gawped, his little pot belly sticking out over his orange shorts. It was nearly as tall as he was, with paper flags sticking out of its slender turrets. There were courtyards and walkways with castellated battlements, bridges that defied gravity and dozens of arched doors and windows, framed with seashells. Best of all were the little action figures that populated it. They were made with the most amazing detail and fixed in all manner of poses: running, crouching, climbing, waving and shouting. It was like they were playing some big game. The sandcastle was utterly amazing and its magnetism pulled him forward another step.

'Hey there little one,' said a voice that drew him up sharp. He looked for its source and saw a fat man slumped in a deckchair. He was wearing a baseball cap and dark sunglasses which sliced through big gingery sideburns. His t-shirt was sky blue with a simple sandcastle print: a crack running down its middle and a little red flag on top. A spade was sticking out of the sand next to him and there was an open rucksack in which Toby could see a plastic water spray, some funny looking tools and a wooden box with a slider lid – the kind his dad kept chess pieces in, only bigger.

'Is this your sandcastle?' he asked.

'Indeed it is.'

'It's really good. I wish I could make one like that.'

The man looked up and down the beach, then back at him. 'Take a closer look if you like, but don't touch the figures.'

Toby didn't need to be asked twice. He got as close as he could without stepping over the walls and circled around it, soaking up its every detail. But it was the figures that fascinated him most. They were nothing like the plastic soldiers he had at home. These looked real. He crouched to look at a little girl who was shouting, marvelling at the detail in her open mouth. He could see all her teeth, the little dots on her tongue and even the dangly bit at the back of her throat. A boy on a battlement above her was waving - his eyes glassy and bright and the lines on his open hand incredibly complex. Even his clothes looked real – right down to the folds on his shorts and the frayed hem of his t-shirt. He was sorely tempted to pick one up, but he didn't want to get in trouble. When he got back around to the front, he thought the man in the deckchair was watching him. It was hard to be certain though, because his sunglasses made it difficult to determine the focus of his gaze.

'Where did you get the figures from?' Toby asked, deciding to put them on his birthday list.

'Made them myself.'

Toby's face stretched longways. 'No wonder you don't want me to touch them. If I made some figures like that, I'd keep them on a shelf and never take them out.'

The man nodded in appreciation of his wisdom. 'Have you seen the hole?' he asked, gesturing with his hand. 'It's the deepest on the beach and I'm hoping to get it all the way down to Australia.' He took a long look to either side then fixed his gaze back on Toby. 'Every kid who visits my sandcastle gets to dig some out... Do you wanna help? You've got good muscles for digging.'

Toby looked down at his sun cream smeared arms with new insight, then feeling suddenly big and strong went to look in the hole. It was nearly as deep as he was tall and there was a disc of water in the bottom.

'Go on,' the Sandcastle Man said, tapping the spade. 'You might be the one to take it through to Australia.'

Toby took a step forward then remembered his mum. He shaded his eyes and looked around, soon picking her out among the deckchairs – still snoozing by the look of it. When he turned back the Sandcastle Man was surveying the beach again.

'Okay. I'll do it mister,' he said brightly, taking up the spade and jumping in with a splash.

He got straight to digging, going at it with the energetic zeal that possesses all children when beginning projects of epic magnitude – head down and wet sand flying off the spade. Less than a minute in, the light in the hole dimmed and his hot back was suddenly aproned with shade. He straightened and almost fell back when he saw the sides of the hole moving away and rising to form great sandy cliffs. The water was rising too and when it reached his knees, he splashed out onto what was now a large beach in front of the cliffs. But the sand under his feet looked like he was viewing it through a magnifying glass. The grains were like the crystals in the salt mill his mum had just bought and when he walked over the surface, he no longer left any footprints. He turned a full circle with his mouth hanging open. High above, wispy clouds drifted across a huge circle of bright blue sky, but the rays of the sun reached only halfway down the sandy cliffs.

'Hey mister!' he called up, surprised by the way his voice echoed around the hole. 'Hey mister!' he tried again louder. 'I think I got down to Australia. But I want to get out now.' When the Sandcastle Man's grinning face appeared over the rim Toby cowered. His head was now the size of a planet and his red sideburns like vast alien jungles.

When he disappeared, Toby sat down against the cliffs and began to cry. He couldn't figure out what had happened. Either he had shrunk like Alice in that story book, or everything had gotten much bigger. He had always thought it would be fun to be in one of those books, but now it was happening, he didn't like it one bit. By now his mum would be wondering where he was. He stood up and called for her repeatedly, tears soon streaming down his face. But she never came.

He waited for what seemed like hours, watching the shade rise on the sunny side of the hole. In the distance, he could hear the amusements and closer by, a blend of voices. But the voices came and went and the vastness of the hole robbed them of clarity. Every so often the brittle cliffs rained sand as someone walked close to the rim and in the end, he decided to sit at the water's edge, fearing a total collapse.

It was getting dark in the hole when the Sandcastle Man appeared again, this time reaching in with a giant arm. Toby ran from his grasping fingers, but there was nowhere to go and he was seized by a vice of monstrous digits. His stomach dropped through his feet as he shot into the sky; the beach suddenly far below him and the hole he had been snatched from, a giant mouth within it. Like the mechanical chair of a fun fair ride, the hand whirled him around; the red and orange lights of the arcades blurring through his vision. He was released onto more of the same coarse sand with his head swimming and fell to all fours. The first thing he saw was a pair of sandaled feet. He got up and found himself looking into the eyes of a girl his own age. Her hands were held out in a warding gesture and her face frozen in a scream. He lurched backwards and struck something hard, spinning to discover another figure – this one a boy, frozen in a run, his face a horrible mask of fear.

Looking around Toby realised he had been dropped onto a walkway of the giant sandcastle, amongst the little figures he had marvelled over. Figures he now realised weren't figures at all, but real children who looked scared to death. Some had raw eyes with tears frozen on

31

their cheeks and others were cowering behind walls and calling for help. He felt a thunderous crash and when he looked over a battlement of sand, he saw crests of huge waves rolling towards him, each crashing against the castle's lower fortifications and eating them away. As he watched, one of the towers on a lower level developed a crack and the front face toppled into the sea.

He looked out across the beach, hoping to see his mum. But to his horror it was almost deserted. The sun was low and the few people who were still there were packing up. His mum was nowhere to be seen and a fresh wave of panic flooded him, setting him off crying anew. Nearby a giant seagull landed with a surprisingly loud flapping of wings and strutted across the sand toward the remnants of someone's packed lunch.

A shadow fell on Toby and he looked up to see the Sandcastle Man looming over him. There was a tray of fish and chips in his hands and he was shovelling them into his mouth with a wooden fork. A slurry of mushy peas fell over the side and slopped down onto the girl whose hands were raised in a warding gesture, turning her green and leaving a giant pea resting on her arms. The Sandcastle Man paused in his gluttony to observe his work and the air erupted with booming laughter.

When another wave shook the castle, Toby knew he had to get off. He had built enough sandcastles on his many trips to the beach to know they were always destroyed by the sea when the tide came in. He saw a set of steps leading to a lower level and rushed down. The walkway at the bottom was wider, but it was cluttered with dozens more frozen children he had to weave around. He saw another set of steps, but as he reached them a colossal finger dropped from the sky, blocking them off. The skin of the finger was nicotine stained and cracked, its ridged nail dirty and shining in the low light of the sun. The Sandcastle Man squatted so his flabby face was level with Toby; the dark moons of his eyes just visible behind his tinted sunglasses. He bit down on a piece of fish batter and the crunch was like a handful of gravel, squeezed in his ear.

Toby ran past the finger and raced onto another stairway, but on the way down the finger came out of nowhere and swiped the bottom half away. He flailed backwards and fell on his bum, saving himself from tumbling headfirst off what was now a six-foot drop onto a lower walkway. The finger withdrew into the sky and a hysterical bout of laughter vibrated his bones.

Nose running and tears streaking his face, he turned onto his tummy and dropped off the broken stairs onto the walkway. This took him to a courtyard with a tower at its centre. A frozen girl was leaning out of a high balcony, her hand raised in a wave to someone a million miles away – like an imprisoned princess in a fairy tale. Around the base of the tower were dozens more children. It had the look of a playground scene when he observed it from his normal size. But in his shrunken form, he realised it was anything but. There were no signs the children were interacting with each another and they all looked stricken by fear and panic – racing away or hiding from an unseen peril. Toby ran through this schoolyard nightmare and onto a sand bridge that led to a lower level, heedless of the cracks that were appearing in it. A big wave struck the castle just as he got across and the whole length fell into a shady chasm between walkways.

This new level had outer walls that were too big to see over and he raced around, soon finding himself back at the bridge with no obvious way out. 'Mum! Mum!' he began to scream, turning one way and the other. 'Please come back. I'm sorry for going off!' The children around him were unmoved by his desperate cries and they continued to stare though him – each trapped in their own eternal horror.

Another wave shook the foundation and spurred him back into action. He went around the same walkway with a red streaming face and had just about given up when he saw an opening in the outer wall he had missed the first time around. It was only waist high and directly behind a crouching girl whose arms were raised as if she were being dazzled by a bright light. He pushed her out of the way with the aid of an adrenaline surge. She was heavy, but once he tilted her far enough she fell away, dropping to her side in the same rigid pose. He squatted in front of the opening and saw it was a tunnel angling down to a circle of daylight about thirty feet away. The sand inside was damp and the air cold, but he ducked and crawled in straight away, his body shivering with fear. The roof collapsed as he reached the other end and he was only just able to pull himself free, wiping sand from his face and spitting out that which had gotten into his mouth. He rose to find himself in a small courtyard and ran up the narrow steps to look over the battlements. The beach ran away for what seemed like miles and the undulations of dry sand higher up the shore looked like the dunes he had seen on T.V. Below him was a hundred-foot drop to the castle moat. Giant waves were crashing into the front defences and surging around the sides. He looked back at the tunnel he had crawled from and back out to sea, realising he had nowhere left to go...

The Sandcastle Man watched with interest, wondering if this one would jump. None of the other children had and most never found the little tunnel to the lowest level. The long drop the boy was looking over was his final challenge and he was starting to think he had made it too high. It was a fall into water, but the drop was probably too big for someone his size. He had waited all afternoon for this – having first watched the boy's hysterical mother and later the police combing the beach for him. A pretty policewoman had even questioned him – standing only three feet from the hole in which the boy was sitting crossed legged by the water. It turned out Toby was his name. He liked to know the names of his figures and this was his first Toby. The policewoman had thanked him for his cooperation and the search was extended to the arcades and ice cream parlours. It was unlikely he would ever feature on their short list of suspects for there were dozens of people who had seen him sitting there all day. He looked around and threw his chip tray onto the sand. The sun was behind the arcades now and most of the beach goers had packed up. If the boy's mum came back next week, she would recognise her son amongst the figures of his next sandcastle. But adults never really looked - only the children did. The adults kept a respectable distance and if they got any closer it was only to pull their children away.

He stepped into the sea and fished out the figures that had already fallen in. He dried them with a tea towel and placed them into his varnished slide box. Three waves later and a crack appeared in the wall beneath the boy, making him jump to one side. The next two waves undermined the battlement completely and it dropped to the sea, taking the boy with it. He fished him out and held him up to the dying sun. His freshly frozen figure was upright with flailing arms – mouth screaming and eyes showing a good deal of white. It was a good pose and quite different from the rest. It all depended on how they were positioned when the waves took them. The next time he built a sandcastle, he would position Toby like a guardian in front of a little bridge.

Watching the frozen ones go into the sea wasn't much fun, so he picked them off the sandcastle, returned them to the box and slid the lid closed. Then, unable to tolerate even the idea of real children playing on his creation, he stomped the castle down to a cluster of soggy mounds. He packed his rucksack with a smile and made his way off the beach.

The Magic Hat

'Hey Pete,' said Chrissie. 'Looks like Bobby dug that magic hat out.'

Pete tore his eyes from the telly and saw his son sitting on the settee with a top hat and wand in his lap. A present they brought back from their romantic weekend away. He remembered how pleased Bobby had been to see them, but also how underwhelmed he'd been with the hat. He had taken it straight to his room and hadn't touched it since. His sudden interest no doubt inspired by the magic show they watched an hour earlier.

Pete sat up and rubbed some life into his face. His parents were round for dinner and for the last hour they had all sunk into their seats with the help of a few glasses of merlot. A few minutes more and he would have been asleep. 'Hey Bobs. You gonna give us a show?' he asked, reaching for the remote control and muting the telly. Bobby's grandparents brightened and shifted on the sofa, glad to have some new stimulation. 'Come into the middle then, so we can see you.'

Bobby took up position in front of the fire. He was wearing checked pyjamas and slippers with Yoda heads for toe boxes. 'Okay. I'm going to make this keyring disappear,' he said, raising an index finger from which a dolphin-tagged keyring dangled.

'Hang on,' said Pete. 'You can't rush into it. You've got to introduce yourself first. Build an atmosphere like The Great Morisimo did.'

Bobby blushed and lowered his arm. 'Good evening everybody,' he said, affecting a deep voice. 'I'm the Incredible Bobby – master of disappearing.' While they laughed, he angled the top hat so everyone could see and rattled the wand around the inside. 'See – nothing there.

No secret compartments or anything.' His Nanna leant forwards, giving it a thorough inspection with screwed up eyes.

Bobby levelled the hat and dropped the keyring in. It struck the bottom with a *clack*. He waved the wand and said, 'Azibizazi!' in that same dramatic tone, at which point Pete and Chrissie exchanged affectionate smiles. Pete hadn't known there was a magic word stitched into the bottom of the hat until after he had given it to Bobby. But his son saw it straight away, holding the inside up to the light and asking what it said. He would have sworn there was no such stitching when he bought it. But then again, he hadn't paid it much attention.

With the magic word fresh out of his mouth, Bobby tapped the hat three times with the wand before angling it to display a now empty interior. Genuinely impressed, they all sat up a little taller and gave him a thunderous round of applause.

'Hey, that's pretty good,' said Pete. 'How'd you do it?'

Bobby was about to answer when Nanna grabbed his arm. 'Don't tell him! A good magician *never* reveals his secrets. If he does, he's not magic anymore.'

'She's right Bobby,' sighed Pete. 'You should keep it to yourself.'

'Okay, it's getting late,' said Chrissie. 'You can have some time reading then we'll be up to tuck you in. Say goodnight to Nanna and Grandad.'

Bobby gave them a big hug and left, slippers whispering on the carpet.

An hour later, with his parents gone and Chrissie in bed, Pete went to tuck Bobby in. 'Lights off now. It's getting late.' Bobby gave him the book he was reading. 'Any good?'

'Yeah. It's about a girl with a limp who can make herself into a ghost.'

'Cool,' he replied, slipping it back into the bookcase. 'What about that trick eh? I bet it took some practice.'

'It's easy Daddy – you just say the magic word and hit it three times. Just like you told me.' His smile dropped and he became suddenly glum. 'But I can't get anything back.'

Pete frowned. 'There must be a secret compartment or something. Have you looked?'

Bobby shook his head.

Pete retrieved the hat from the shelf and felt around the inside. And apart from the stitched letters of the magic word, he felt nothing but smooth black velvet. He picked at the disk of material in the base, hoping to expose a false bottom. When he didn't find one, he brought his other hand to the bottom, gauging its thickness. A few millimetres at most. 'What did you put in?'

'Some marbles and that dolphin keyring...That little torch you got me for Christmas and the fire engine.'

'The Lego fire engine I helped you to build?'

'Yep.'

'No way. You can't have. That's too big to be hidden in here...' He looked at his son's innocent face and smiled, finally understanding that he was being taken for a fool.

'Why don't you make something else disappear and I'll get it straight back for you,' said Pete, expecting Bobby to make some squirmy excuse as to why it wouldn't work. But he didn't. He sat up against his headboard, seemingly enthused by the idea.

'Alright Daddy. What shall we use? I don't want to use any good stuff in case you can't get them back.'

Pete laughed. He dug into his pockets and pulled out a piece of scraggy tissue. 'This'll do,' he said and tossed it in. Bobby pulled the hat onto his lap and without even bothering to screen the interior, spoke the magic word and struck the hat three times with the wand. On the third stroke the tissue vanished.

Pete stared.

'Get it back then Daddy.'

He looked at his son, then back into the hat, the pleasant intoxication of several red wines now a distant memory. *'No way!'*

Bobby beamed. 'It's good, isn't it?'

Pete took the hat and felt around the inside again. Tipped it... shook it. 'It's vanished.'

'I know. It's a magic hat.'

'Do it with this,' said Pete, taking a ten pence piece from his wallet.

Bobby repeated the trick and the coin vanished on the third strike of the wand.

'Never,' said Pete, giving the hat another silent shake.

'Well Daddy. Are you gonna get it back then?'

'I don't think I can. It didn't come with any instructions, but I'll take it tonight and try figuring it out.' Bobby looked disappointed. Enough so that he didn't notice how pale his father's face was. 'Come on now. Lie down and shut your eyes.'

Pete turned the bedside light off and when Bobby slid under the covers, he kissed him goodnight and left.

He went through to his bedroom where his wife was also reading in bed. He closed the door and placed the top hat on his pillow. 'You've got to look at this and tell me I haven't gone crazy.'

Chrissie put her book down with an irritated smile, raising her eyebrows in the manner of a long-suffering wife.

'Just watch,' he said, picking up the closest thing to hand and dropping it in - a black ballpoint that was lying next to his alarm clock. He said the magic word tapped the side of the hat three times and the pen disappeared.

'Wow!' said Chrissie.

'See. *Now* you're interested.' She took the hat from him and went through an almost identical inspection to the one he performed five minutes earlier.

'Go on then,' she said at last. 'Tell me how you did it.'

He met her eyes - his face grave in the extreme. 'That's just it. It's not a trick. It really disappeared.'

'Yeah right,' she said, retrieving her book. 'It's good though, I'll give you that.'

'Try it yourself. Come on Chrissie humour me.'

'Alright.' She flung the covers back, went to her dressing table and brought back an almost empty tube of moisturiser and dropped it in. She took the wand and was about to tap the hat when he grabbed her wrist. 'Say the magic word first.'

'*Really?*'

'Yes really. Say Azibizazi first, then tap it three times.'

'How many drinks did you have?'

'Same as you. Come on. Please.'

'Okay. Azibizazi.' She tapped the hat with the wand, counting the strokes. 'One, two, three.' When the tube of moisturiser blinked out of existence she recoiled with a sharp intake of breath. More shocked than he had been. And after a few seconds of just staring, she picked the hat up and shook it.

'I don't like it... How can it disappear like that?' She looked at him with dawning recollection. 'Remember that creepy man who sold it to us? The one who made my skin crawl.'

Pete remembered alright. It was on their return from their romantic weekend away. They had forgotten to buy Bobby a gift and had nipped into town before going home. They ended up in Market Vaults - the underground warren of independent shops beneath Scarborough Market. They wandered the brown flagstone aisles, dipping in and out of several shops and coming finally to the far corner of the vaults and a shop called Enzo's Emporium. Its little windows were covered with dense black lace and the arched doorway fitted with velvet curtains that obstructed the view of the interior. The sign in the window said open, but the only way of seeing inside was to push through. They looked at each other, shrugged and went in. The inside was furnished with several trestle tables endowed with the same disappointing mix of second-hand items you could find at any car boot sale: porcelain animals, action figures, keyrings and lighters; toy soldiers and beer mats, bangles and wallets. The reason for the curtains, now painfully obvious. They browsed the first table and wrinkled their noses. But as they turned to go, the proprietor stepped through the doorway, blocking the only exit.

'Hello, my friends,' he said, welcoming them with wide arms. He was a big man with a grey flecked beard and a white open-necked shirt with top hat cuff links. Pete thought he recognised him but couldn't think from where.

'Welcome to Enzo's Emporium. Find something you want and Enzo will give you a good price.'

Pete's heart sank as the man began picking up items and extolling their virtues. 'How about a wallet? This one's got a press stud compartment for change and a flip out card holder.' When Pete shook his head, he picked a necklace from over a dozen displayed on a red velvet cushion. 'A silver locket then, to compliment the lady's sparkling eyes.' Before Chrissie could say a word, he stepped into her personal space, opening the item as if meaning to fasten it about her neck. But she stepped away, warding him off with a gesture that strained politeness. The man took no offence and simply smiled, displaying a row of brilliant white teeth. 'Perhaps if I knew what you're looking for.'

'Something for my son,' Pete said, regretting the words as soon as they were out. *We're just browsing* would have been better.

Enzo's eyes lit up. 'Then you've come to the right place.' He whirled, doing a full rotation and snatching up a large black top hat and wand. 'Your boy likes magic eh?'

'Suppose so,' Pete said. He wanted to leave, but the proprietor remained in the doorway.

'Name a fair price and Enzo won't haggle.'

Pete looked at Chrissie. 'What do you think? We could spend all day looking for something.'

'Just buy it and let's get out of here.'

He dug into his wallet and pulled a tenner out.

'More than fair,' Enzo said, plucking it out of his hand before any price was agreed and swapping it for the top hat and wand. Then he stepped aside and held the curtain open for them. 'To make something disappear, just tell him to say the magic word and tap the hat three times.'

'Will do,' said Pete as they squeezed by and through the curtain. He hadn't asked about the magic word and they only found out what it was when Bobby showed them the gold stitching.

'What are we going to do?' asked Chrissie. 'Shall we call the police?'

Pete laughed. 'You're kidding, right?'

'Whatever you do – I want it out of this house right now. It's creeping me out.'

'I don't want to throw it in the bin.'

'Take it out back and burn it then. I don't want it anywhere near me.'

Pete took it downstairs, but when he reached the back door, he hesitated on the handle. Getting rid of it seemed like a good idea, but there was bound to be people who would pay good money for it. And how could he let it go without showing it to his mates? He was going to the Crown Tavern for a few jars tomorrow and he could imagine their faces when he started making stuff disappear. Might even be a way he could make a few quid. There was no denying the hat's creepiness and he felt odd just holding it. He would get rid of it, but not yet. So, instead of taking it outside, he put it in the boiler cupboard, on top of the board games. He would put it in his car in the morning, take it to pub after work and dispose of it afterwards. He shut the cupboard and went to bed, telling Chrissie it was all sorted.

The next morning, Bobby woke him by jumping on the bed. 'It's a bit early Bobs. Go down and watch some telly for a bit. You know how to turn it on.' His son said something undiscernible and left. He was drifting back to sleep when he sensed him in the room again. He heard him whisper something to Chrissie who spoke back in a tone that froze his blood, 'Get that off right now!'

Pete jerked up to see Bobby standing at the foot of the bed, wearing the top hat.

'I don't want to take it off,' he said pushing his fists down and sloping his shoulders. 'I want to wear it like the magic man.'

'Well you can't. Tell him Pete!'

'Do what your mother says.'

Bobby looked at him. 'Do I look like The Great Morisimo Daddy?'

 Before he could reply, Bobby said the magic words and tapped his hat three times. The instant the wand struck for the third time, his son disappeared. The hat and wand hung in the air for several seconds then dropped to the floor.

Chrissie screamed, Pete gasped and they both jumped out of bed. She dropped to her knees to look under the bed, lifting the bottom of the blankets to look underneath.

'What just happened!? she shrieked. 'Where's he gone? Where's he gone Pete?' But he couldn't answer. His body had taken on the consistency of drying cement and all he could do was stare at the place his son had disappeared. 'Bobby! Where are you?' she shrieked again, pulling cupboards open with wild eyes. She even snatched the hat up, looking inside as if she would find him there. She flung it into the corner, grabbed Pete's collar and began beating his chest. 'Where's he gone? I thought you burnt that thing.' Pete's mouth moved, but all he could do was stare. She pushed him away in disgust and ran to Bobby's room, imploring him to come out and telling him she wouldn't be mad.

She thundered back in and shoved him in the back. 'Why are you just standing there? Find him!'

'He's gone, just like everything else.'

His wife reeled, twisting one way then the other, like a broken robot with no direction.

'We've got to follow him,' she said, and it didn't dawn on Pete what she meant until she snatched the wand from the floor and put the hat on her head.

'No! Don't!' He made a grab for her, but she side stepped around the bed. Her face was white, her eyes those of a banshee. He made another attempt on her, but she leapt onto the bed, the word Azibizazi passing her lips in a wavering cry. She tapped the hat three times and disappeared. And this time the hat and wand stayed in place for what seemed like an eternity before falling to the bed.

Pete dropped to his knees on the blankets. His hands were shaking, his body a hollow shell he no longer inhabited. There was a feeling of something sweeping up to consume him – a madness he could never escape. He sensed his last lucid seconds slipping away and made his decision. Family was everything and wherever Chrissie and Bobby had gone, he had to follow. He doffed the hat and in a voice that surprised him in its confidence, he spoke the magic word and struck the hat three times.

He came to as if rising from darkness. He once had a back operation for which he needed a general anaesthetic and his return to the world was not dissimilar. Only he wasn't returning from the oblivion of intravenous propofol. He was rising from the spiralling blackness at the bottom of the hat.

He felt hardness beneath him… the weight of his lolling head… tightness around his thighs, calves and forearms. He opened his eyes to near darkness, the only light generated by a green exit sign and a red bulb. He was strapped to a chair and there was something on his head that felt like a dish. He tried to call out, but he was gagged with thick cloth that smelt of turps and sweaty socks. He struggled for a time, but his restraints were expertly applied and chaffing was the only reward for his efforts. He heard a scream and froze. It was followed by laughter and voices. Beyond that the sound of... arcade machines? Nearer still a muffled voice... maybe two, someone else trying to speak through a gag, perhaps calling to him. Chrissie and Bobby? Disorientation reigned. The last thing he remembered was putting Bobby's hat on, and that felt like weeks ago...

The voices grew nearer and there was a click from somewhere off to his right. Weak light cut into the room as a door burst open and a row of people filed in behind floor-to-ceiling bars. A precession of people, distinctly cautious in their movements. Some holding one another – others bunching in tight knots. The door closed and for a few seconds everything went dark again. A pregnant silence ensued, interrupted by nervous giggling. Suddenly everything was blindingly bright and Pete was contorting in his chair - agonizing electricity lancing through his body. He would have screamed, but his jaw would only clench against his grimy gag. When it passed, he slumped in the chair – his prior agony instantly mocked and applauded from the other side of the bars.

The lights went out and a spotlight came on, illuminating a woman slumped with her hands tied behind her back. The rope that bound her was attached to a winch that began winding, pulling her arms up behind her. Forcing her to her feet and then onto tiptoes. The winch kept going, lifting her clean off the floor and dislocating her shoulders. A gag dampened her screams, but her legs did a good job of illustrating her pain – in the way they kicked the air in search of support. The audience laughed, but this time several turned away – unable to look at the extreme angle of the woman's arms. Chrissie! Pete realised when the rope twisted, turning her tortured face to the light.

Now the spotlight swung to focus on a rack upon which little Bobby was stretched out, his eyes bulging with terror as the winch on *his* apparatus began to wind. Creaking ropes tightened on his delicate wrists and ankles – stretching him to his physiological limit and lifting him clear. Yoda slippers falling into darkness. His muffled wail pierced Pete's heart like a stake, each terrible note driving it ever deeper. With tears streaming his face, Pete called to the spectators through his spit-soaked gag, pleading for someone to help his son. But they couldn't hear. To them, this was harmless entertainment and when the spotlight blinked off they giggled in the darkness, leaving by another door when the red light turned green.

When Pete heard distant arcades again, he realised he was in The Charnel House – the new horror experience on the sea front. He'd visited with Chrissie at Halloween and remembered being in this very room – looking through the bars from the other side. And later, over drinks, agreeing that the actor's screams had sounded so real. Their terror, so authentic.

Overhead strip lights came on and a man stepped in. He was wearing a top hat just like Bobby's and he looked the part of a Victorian magician. Pete had seen this man outside The Charnel House in various horror costumes, scaring teenagers in a bid to attract them in. And it was the same man from Enzo's Emporium.

Enzo paced the room, studying them like artwork. 'You did good,' he said finally, addressing them like actors in a play. 'People want realism and that's what you gave them. Automated dummies don't cut it anymore.' He turned to Chrissie, who was back on the floor now, sobbing with pain. 'There's no need for tears young lady. Enzo looks after his staff. There are other rooms than this and I intend to rotate you. If it's any consolation, there's only three months of the season left. After that, it's back in the hat.' He crouched next to Bobby. 'And don't worry about your Lego fire engine little man. It's in my shop with the other toys and it won't be long before someone gives it a new home.'

It occurred to Pete as he looked into his son's wet, pleading eyes, that there hadn't been anything of any size for sale in Enzo's Emporium. Everything had been small enough to fit into a magician's hat.

Enzo doffed his hat and did a full turn with its interior tipped towards them. 'A voice operated, password-protected wormhole connecting *your* top hat to mine. Genius eh? I'm sure Einstein would agree. Must admit though, you clogged it up some – the three of you coming through one after the other like that. Had an awful time getting you out. But you're here now so not to worry.' He looked at his watch. 'Time to go, but I'll be watching. We're open till ten and if you do well, it'll be fish and chips for supper. You've got to keep your strength for a job like this.'

He left by the door under the green light and in the ensuing darkness Pete struggled once more against his bindings, firing muffled expletives into his gag. In the end he sagged with exhaustion, drawing huge breaths through the filthy material. He remembered the other things he'd seen in The Charnel House: a woman being lowered into a vat of hot oil, a man with his feet held to a fire and a boy in thumb screws. Their terror had been real and like the others he had stood spectator to their agonies and laughed them off. Later giving the experience a five-star review on Trip Advisor. And with that he began to cry, regretting his decision to keep the hat and thinking about what might lay in store for his wife and little boy.

Daylight Robbery

Dave was four fingers down his fifth pint when he saw Tommo weaving through the bar stools.

'Now then Davey Boy,' Tommo said, clicking his glass down. 'Mind if I join you?'

He swept his hand at the empty seats. 'Take your pick.'

Tommo sat, one knee jigging up and down. 'Heard you split with Susie.'

'That's right.'

'Shit. You two were tight.'

'Yeah well. I don't wanna talk about it... You still in the game?'

'Not anymore. Been straight for six months. Even doing a bit of charity work.'

'Bollocks.'

'Seriously. I'm on a project this week in Peasholm Park. De-sludging that little stream.'

Dave took a closer look at Tommo, registering now what he hadn't noticed before. His old partner was clean shaven and bereft of bling. His speech, unusually coherent for ten o'clock on a Saturday night. 'Good for you.'

'How about you? Still doing a bit?'

'Now and again. When needs must.'

Tommo leaned in. 'Good, cos I've got a tip for you.'

'Thought you was out of it.'

'I am. But if I was still going, I'd be doing the place myself. I was looking it over before I packed in. An old house at the back end of Scalby - isolated with no alarms. Owner's minted. Big in psychology from what I gather. Wrote some papers on criminal reform of all things... Interested?'

'Might be.'

Tommo whispered the address and slapped him on the back before returning to his friends.

The next morning Dave woke with a hangover and after a stiff coffee decided to drive to Susie's and offer to take her out for lunch. As friends – to talk things over. He'd never been any good at relationships and they all seemed to end up functioning like apparatus in a play park. Some went round and round, others swung back and forth or see-sawed up and down. With Susie it was more like a big slide, climbing to a great height before plunging into a muddy puddle when she found out he was burgling again. Breaking the solemn promise he'd made on their second anniversary. But, despite her expletive-laced vow to never have anything to do with him again, he still had hope.

He was halfway to her little garden flat when he decided to take a detour through Scalby - to check out the address Tommo had given him. He knew the approximate location of the house and he slowed on his approach. It was screened by a tall privet hedge, but he got a decent look when he passed the driveway. A detached red-and-white Victorian gaff with an ivy entwined portico, fronted by a huge lawn and a dazzling flower bed. Interest piqued, he pulled up where the road crested a hill and got out, pretending to clean his back window while stealing a peek into the property's rear garden. It stretched back over a hundred yards to a hedge, beyond which was a swathe of thick woodland.

He drove to the next T-junction, took a left and pulled into a dirt layby. He kept a change of clothes in the boot that he used to scout places out: grey joggers, black t-shirt and baseball cap. He changed and jogged alongside the woodland at the back of the house, soon taking a trail into the trees. A short way in, he encountered an elderly lady walking two dogs. He raised a hand but ducked his head so the peak of his cap covered the upper half of his face as he puffed by – becoming, he hoped, a non-descript jogger that would arouse no suspicion.

He saw the back of the house through a break in foliage and stopped with his hands on his hips as if catching his breath. He looked around to be sure he was alone, then left the track, pushing through the vegetation to the back of the house. Several minutes later, his arm scratched in several places, he arrived at the hawthorn hedgerow that separated the woodland from the property's rear garden. At first glance it looked impenetrable, but after a bit of ducking and sidling he found a weakness in the corner – a natural gap that, besides raking him with a few twigs, would admit him well enough. He decided to bring some cutters with him next time and turned to leave. In doing so he realised the corner was screened from the house by a row of fir trees on the other side and on impulse he decided it wouldn't hurt to push through now.

He spent some time listening for signs of occupancy, before inching through, cringing at the rustling he produced. A sound that felt monstrous against the quiet of the woods. If anyone caught him, he would tell them he had left the track to take a leak. Got turned around in the foliage and saw a short cut through the garden to the main road. Lame, but plausible.

Free of the hedge and now most certainly trespassing, he crept to the nearest tree and peered through its needled branches. He was a good ninety yards from the rear of the house, separated by a lawn that was due a good cutting. A patio ran the width of the house, surrounded by a breezeblock wall topped with resplendent flower boxes. He saw now how easy it would be to reach that wall and take a closer look through the windows. All he had to do was follow the tree line and run five yards of open ground.

What!? Are you crazy? It's broad daylight. Get the fuck out before anyone sees you!

It was the voice of reason, but for some reason its authority was questionable – like a drill sergeant barking orders in ladies' underwear. He started to turn, but his feet were rooted. Thing was - he didn't think anyone was going to see him. There didn't appear to be any cameras and the house *felt* empty. He wasn't sure where the feeling was coming from, but he suspected it was the intuitive radar he had developed through many years of experience. So, instead of retreating, he hurried along the firs and made a dash for the patio wall, sticking his head up between flowerpots to survey the windows. Looking for signs of habitation and a way in. For several minutes he remained perfectly still – becoming ever more confident no one was home. A look through the window wouldn't hurt – long enough to get an idea of what might be inside. Then he would leave.

In full burglar mode he jumped the patio wall and pressed himself against the house's cool brickwork, edging sideways until he could see into the kitchen. Quartz worktops and copper tiles; posh pans hanging above a central island. Curved cupboards and a butler sink. A top dollar instalment by the look of it, boding well for what lay beyond. Without thinking, his hand went to the patio doors, depressed the handle and pushed it open. He jerked back – not quite believing what he had done.

Too confident you idiot!

In his line of work, confidence had to be kept trim like fingernails. Let it grow too long and you were liable to get a strip torn off. But that chastising voice was even weaker now. He crossed the threshold and listened to the inside of the house as he stared at the gleaming tiles.

Leaving the door open for a quick getaway, he ventured further, trainers whispering on the wooden floor. A door to his right was ajar and he crept over, inching it open on a dark garage. He felt up the wall and flicked the light on. The space was filled top to bottom with tools, most of which looked brand new. Many were wall mounted and there were dozens of neatly labelled drawers filled with fixings. Garden tools, steps, a three-piece ladder and a lawn mower. It had the look of a DIY store minus the counter and price tags. And there were no marks on the concrete floor to suggest a vehicle had ever been stored there. He switched the light off and followed the hall to a huge lounge that looked onto the drive, its windows fitted with heavy brocade curtains in a flower design. Looking around, it occurred to him there was something seriously wrong. No TV. What kind of person has no TV? Two sofas and a reclining chair all faced a coffee table at the centre of the room - one made from an old barrel with a built-in chessboard. There was a bookshelf running the length of one wall. Bookshelves weren't new to him, but his family and friends used them for ornaments and DVDs. These were packed with books – so precisely that when he took one out there was slight resistance to its removal and a pleasant slipping sound. The Case for Restorative Justice was its title. He flicked through the pages and slipped it back without interest. He walked along the shelf reading spines: Criminal Psychology, The Making of a Murderer, Juvenile Delinquency and its Causes, Offender Profiling. They were all about crime and its causes and he wondered what the owner would think to know a career criminal was browsing his shelves. He stood behind the sofa to survey the room once more. Someone with this kind of money could easy afford a 60-inch OLED with surround sound, but had chosen to fill it with books and a chessboard. He could mount it on the chimney stack, right where a stupid portrait had been hung. A portrait depicting an elderly man who had to be the owner. He held his hands out to the room and shook his head at the image, as if to say *What were you thinking?* Money it appeared, couldn't buy taste.

The doorbell rang and he jumped – full panic mode swamping his system. He was caught in the lounge and there was no way out. If there was anyone upstairs, they would surely see him as he fled through the hall. Fuck. What did he think he was doing? He pressed himself into the corner of the bay window, hoping he couldn't be seen from the doorway. When the bell rang for a second time and no one answered, he began to relax. An empty house after all. He stayed in place for a full minute before risking a look out of the window. To his relief the visitor had departed, but there was a box on the doorstep. A box with a big white label on top.

He became instantly curious as to what was inside and went to the front door. He tried the handle. Unlocked. For someone who thought so much about crime, the owner sure was sloppy about locking up. With the door cracked open, he scanned the driveway before stepping out and snatching the box inside. The label was an invoice and the box wasn't sealed - its cardboard flaps folded in on one another. Left then by someone who knew the owner. He eased the flaps open and viewed the contents: a tin of blue paint, a packet of fine sandpaper, a bag of tap washers and a green jerry can full of petrol. Nothing to vindicate the strange and sudden curiosity that had driven him to bring the box inside.

He puffed his disappointment and chastised himself for losing focus. *Christ!* What was wrong with him today? He shouldn't even be in the house – let alone be taking the owner's shopping in. If he got collared for such idiocy he would never forgive himself. He deserved to get caught, playing silly buggers like this. He made to leave, but the idea of taking such risks and leaving empty-handed narked him. He was here now and for all the risk, he might as well get something in return. A little cash or jewellery would do just fine, and such things were usually hidden upstairs.

He bounded up onto the landing. The first door he came to was standing open on a single bedroom that didn't appear to be in use. The bed was made with hospital corners and there was a framed picture on the drawers – of a lad of about twelve, dressed in school uniform. He went to the next room and almost whistled at the huge corner bath and the ornate his-and-hers basin. Perfect except for the dripping tap. A drip amplified by the tiled floor and walls.

The next room was the master bedroom. The wardrobes were mirrored and the sudden sight of himself brought him up sharp. He was an experienced burglar – but seeing himself creeping around the bed in full burglar mode was unsettling. No darkness to hide in - just the truth of his life choices, reflected back to him in broad daylight. It made him think of what it would be like to be caught on CCTV and to have to sit in a police interview room while the footage was played. He'd read somewhere that shop workers were less likely to steal from a till if there was mirror glass on the wall behind it. He had sniffed at the article, but as he looked at his own furtive reflection, he thought there might be something in it. He tore his eyes from the mirror and felt his thieving instincts return. Whoever owned this gaff could afford to lose some small change and was probably insured up the arse. What he was doing was proactive socialism – redistributing wealth without the need for taxation.

He found a safe built into the wall at the back of a wardrobe and shook his head in frustration. He was no safebreaker, but he pulled the handle in reflex and was surprised when the door swung open, revealing three rolls of banknotes, a little pot of gold rings and a watch. Jackpot! And on the shelf beneath was a rolled-up money bag, big enough to hold it all. As he stuffed it all in, he noticed a photo of the owner fixed on the wall above the safe. It was a strange place for such a picture and he thought again of the research on mirror glass, wondering if this was a variation. Showing the face of the victim to a robber while he was committing the crime. Nice trick, but he wasn't falling for it. If the man didn't want robbing, he should start by locking his doors and his safe. There would no doubt be something in the paper about this robbery – an article that would sympathize with the owner. More appropriate would be an article with the headline:

Careless Rich Guy Loses Savings to Daylight Robber. But they'd never print that.

He hurried out, but as he passed the bathroom he heard the dripping tap and went in to stare at the teardrops of water forming on the tap and falling into the basin. A dripping tap had been the trigger for one of the worst arguments he'd had with Susie. Such a simple problem that had somehow escalated into a full-blown shouting match during which he told her that *she* was like a dripping tap, the way she was going on. *Drip, drip, fucking drip*, had been his exact words – a line swiftly answered in the form of a loaded ashtray flying towards his head. He got his arms up just in time and it clocked painfully off his elbow, leaving a huge bruise that lasted weeks.

'I've been asking you to fix it for months,' she'd said. 'Not like you've got other things to do. Lying on that sofa all day and watching TV. What good are you if you can't fix a sodding tap!?'

He opened the cupboard under the sink and squatted down, spying a service valve behind a bottle of hand wash.

You're not thinking of fixing it are you?

But that inner voice was a frail whisper now – pushed down by a much stronger narrative.

'I can fix a tap,' he said to himself, Susie's weeks old comment, suddenly an affront to his manhood, requiring urgent remedy.

He went to the box in the hall and removed the washers, took the necessary tools from the garage and set about the repair. His every action confident and competent, despite never having fixed a tap in his whole life.

You've fucking lost it man! his inner voice screamed. *Lost it big style!*

There – all done.

He gathered his tools and left, but at the top of the steps he glanced into the single bedroom, straight at the picture on the drawers. The lad was the same age as Georgie - the son he hadn't seen in a long time. Not that he had been denied access or anything – he just hadn't bothered. His mother Hannah had shacked up with some new guy who wore suits to work. Georgie called him Dad now. By the look of the room it wasn't in occupancy and he guessed the boy was the owner's grandchild, who probably stayed over on weekends. He went in and opened the cupboard, finding a PlayStation and a deflated football under empty hangers.

When he turned back, the boy in the picture was now Georgie – judging him with his deep blue eyes. Even when they lived together, he had spent little time with his kid – preferring to be at the gym or down the pub with his mates. And whenever he was left with the boy, it was always a chore. If he took him to the park, he would slump on a bench, staring into his phone while he climbed frames and flew down slides, lifting his face with great reluctance when his calls of *Watch this Daddy!* became too irritating.

He once bought him a train set for Christmas, but got so pissed he fell asleep after promising to set it up. Georgie tried to fix it together while he dribbled in a chair, and in his enthusiasm, broke one of the tracks. He woke with a sore head and on discovering the broken track, shouted until Georgie cried, causing a fallout with his mum and spoiling Christmas for another year. On his fifth birthday the kid asked for his room decorating with dinosaur wallpaper. He'd told him it was too expensive and asked him to choose something different. Truth was, he couldn't be arsed to put it up. All that stripping and pasting - too much like hard work. The lad got a toy helicopter instead, but hardly touched it. He spent that week covering his torn woodchip with dinosaur drawings he never once praised him for. He wasn't the fathering type so when Hannah took off to her mum's with the boy, he'd didn't fight. He saw now what a bastard he'd been and the shame perfused him in a way it had never been able to. And now more than anything, he wished he could put things right.

He looked around at the yellow walls and thought about the pot of blue paint in the box he'd brought in – definitely more of a boy's colour. He couldn't go back and change things with Georgie, but he could put a smile on this boy's face when he next visited. He pulled the furniture into the centre of the room, found some paint brushes and dustcovers in the garage and brought them up along with the paint and sandpaper. He saw a bike pump with an adaptor that looked like it would fit the football and brought that too. He gave the wall a light sanding and set about painting, each stroke of the brush assuaging his simmering regret. By the time he was done, his arm was aching like crazy and he realised he'd done all the walls without taking a break. He pumped the ball up, swept the room and returned the tools and paint to the garage. Washed the brushes and placed them back on the rack.

Feeling good, he left the house by the kitchen, but he got no further than the patio. He looked at the grass, thinking again how it was badly in need of a mowing. As a young lad in need of pocket money he once went from door to door offering to do odd jobs for a small price. He'd washed an old lady's car and cleaned a pregnant mother's windows. But there was this old man who walked with a frame and who offered him 50p to mow his back lawn. He had been quick to agree, but it had been one of those old push mowers and the work was back breaking. When he was done, he returned to the house where the old man asked if he'd included the little patch of grass behind the apple trees. He hadn't. But he said he had and took the money, knowing he'd be long gone before the old bag of bones discovered his deceit. He spent the 50p on football stickers and sweets. But he felt bad about lying and for the next week he kept imagining the old man's disappointment.

He remembered the lawnmower he'd seen in the garage - a petrol driven monstrosity that would make easy work of the lawn. He went back for a second look, taking the jerry can with him. He had an inkling the fuel had been ordered for the lawnmower and he smiled when he saw the arrow on its fuel gauge pointing to empty. He topped it up and crossed to the roll shutter doors – hand hovering over the green button that opened them.

You're not going to mow that lawn are you? Get a grip! The rattle of those shutters and the rumble of that mower will have the whole neighbourhood over here!

But that was exactly what he was going to do and he knew with absolute certainty he would feel better afterwards. He pressed the button and as the shutters juddered upwards, he wheeled the mower to the back of the house as if he had every right to be there. He went straight to work and was soon engrossed, the smell of grass cuttings sweetening the air. The sun on his back and his t-shirt damp with sweat. For the next hour he was a boy again, mowing that old man's garden and doing his best. And by the time he finished, there were a dozen professional looking lines in the grass.

He returned to himself then, the bizarre nature of his last few hours breaking into his psyche. *I've gotta get out of here,* he thought, horrified by his lapse. He went inside to retrieve his money bag and was suddenly gripped by euphoria – the deeds he had done affecting him like a drug. And by the time he reached for the money, he realised taking it would undermine those deeds, and more importantly, his high. On impulse, he took the money bag to the master bedroom and emptied the contents back into the safe. Then, after a moment's hesitation, he added his own watch and all the paper money from his wallet. He shut the safe, replaced the bag on the shelf and left. As he passed the empty box in the hall, he paused to pick up the invoice, realising that having someone finance his deeds would diminish them as much as taking the money. And now more than anything, he needed complete ownership of them.

He whipped his phone out and dialled the number on the invoice. It rang three times before being answered. 'Remedial Supplies. How may I help you?'

'I've got an invoice I wanna settle – ref: CH9714. With credit card if it's ok.'

'Give me a minute... Alright. I've got you down for eighty-five pounds and fifty-nine pence. Is that right sir?'

'It is... But I'd like to add a tip.'

'That's very kind of you. How much?'

'Make it a round hundred.'

'Very generous sir. Long number off the front please.' Dave gave the number and waited patiently for the payment to be processed. 'That's all gone through. Anything else I can help you with?'

'No that's... Wait, yes there is as a matter of fact.' He thought about a stain he'd seen on the lounge carpet, some discoloured grouting in the shower and some scuffed wood in the kitchen. 'Can I place another order?'

'Go ahead.'

'A bottle of carpet cleaner, some white shower grouting and a small pot of floor stain – dark oak.'

'Very good. I'll drop it off at the required time.'

Dave shoved his phone back in his pocket and smiled, feeling better than ever.

The next Friday he was back in town again, having decided to visit one of his old haunts. He saw Jeff come in with his new friends and went over to talk.

'So, you still doing a bit?' Dave asked when there was no one in earshot.

'Now and again. You?'

'Packed it in last week. Swore an oath never to go back. But there's this place in Scalby I had my eye on – banged full of loot and with no security. And for old time's sake, I'll give you the address...'

Torupsun's Panoply of Keys

Stan left the bakery and headed home, munching on his chocolate flapjack. It was his third visit in as many days. But as good as their flapjacks were, it was the new girl that kept him going back. He had planned to talk to her today, but the shop had filled up behind him and he bottled it. All he knew about her was her name and he'd gotten that from her badge.

He slowed as he passed a shop that was boarded up last week. The boards were down now and it looked amazing. The window had a decorative wrought iron surround from which all manner of keys projected inwards. A bespoke piece that must have cost a fortune. On a panel above, the shop's name was written in black letters on a red background: *Torupsun's Panoply of Keys*. Stan stepped up to the window to look inside, but the sun was out and the glass was reflecting the street. He considered pressing his face to the window and cupping his eyes, but it would be embarrassing if someone was looking out from the other side. So he decided to take a proper look instead, finishing his flapjack and stepping inside.

The interior looked more like a lock-and-key museum than a shop and for a time he just stood in the doorway, not sure how to proceed. The room was furnished with rows of walnut display cases and a counter that ran diagonally across the far corner. The walls were whitewashed brick; hung with key-themed artwork and tapestries. There were several racks of keys on the counter and a hefty machine he assumed to be a key cutter. A key shop then. But there was nothing tacky about it. No novelty keyrings, lighters, or discount umbrellas. A tall man, he assumed to be the proprietor was at the counter, engaged in a discussion with a young couple. He glanced over and raised his hand in greeting.

Stan went to the nearest cabinet to look at an illustration of an old-fashioned key that had all its parts labelled. The part you took hold of was labelled the bow and the long middle section, the shaft. The business end was the pin and bit. He made his way down the aisle scanning a succession of key cabinets. Hidden lights illuminated the interiors and each collection's name was engraved in an ornate top panel – Egyptian, Roman, Greek, Byzantine and Viking. The keys were all displayed on delicate mounts, below which printed cards detailed their age, composition and usage. Most were functional keys – used for doors, chests and cupboards. But there was a scattering of ceremonial, decorative and votive ones too. Most were stylish, with elaborate bows and barrel ornamentation. Some were said to double as hairpins, and there was one with a dagger-like projection that could be turned on a would-be mugger. There were several twelfth century amulet keys that warded against evil; one with a cruciform bow that could open a church organ. There were some ugly keys with crude hanging loops and dainty ones that looked fit for royal music boxes. In amongst them were keys that didn't look like keys at all. Baffling ones that looked like old-fashioned ring-pulls and intricate ones that looked like metallic origami; created by someone on an acid trip. Most were made of copper, bronze or iron, but some were a composite of two metals. And in one cabinet there were some really old ones made of wood. The Roman cabinet had several figural keys on display - pretentious chunks of metal that spoke of wealthy owners and vaults of treasure. There was a ram's head with ruby eyes, a closed fist and a phallus; an alligator snout and a soaring eagle. At the end of the row Stan raised his head to take in the whole room. It was an impressive and no doubt valuable collection, and he wondered at the wisdom of opening such a place without any security.

He stepped aside to allow the couple to exit, then went to look at a painting. A typical renaissance piece by the looks of it, set in a baroque frame. It depicted a group of men gathered in front of a temple in a large piazza. Jesus was in the foreground and he was handing a pair of keys to a kneeling man.

'Ah, Perugino's *Christ Handing the Keys to Saint Peter*,' said the shopkeeper, appearing by his side. 'Inspired by Matthew 16:19 "And I will give unto thee the keys of the kingdom of heaven; and whatsoever thou shalt bind on earth shall be bound in heaven; and whatsoever thou shalt loose on earth shall be loosed in heaven." The gold key represents his power to dissolve any sin and open the door to heaven and eternal life. The silver one – the power to lock out unworthy souls from the gates of heaven… Who knows where those keys are now, but they'd be a welcome addition to my collection.'

Stan gave him a sideways smile, not sure if he was taking the piss. 'Are those the same keys?' he asked, spotting a plush red banner with two similar crossed keys.

'No. They're different,' said the shopkeeper. 'That's the coat of arms of the Holy See. A newly consecrated pope is given two diagonally crossed keys of gold and silver which are buried with him on his death. In this case the silver key represents the authority of the pope and the gold key the power of heaven.'

'You know a lot about keys.'

'As you'd expect,' he said, holding his hand out. 'Name's Torupsun.'

'Stan,' he replied and shook. The shopkeeper was a tall streak of a man with corduroy trousers and braces. Immaculate white shirt with black key-shape cuff links. 'I've never seen a shop like this before.'

'That's because there aren't any. Surprising really, given how important keys are. Keys represent opening and closing powers; knowledge and success. In one context they symbolise freedom and liberation; in another, incarceration and slavery.'

'Hmmm. I've never given them much thought.'

'Most people don't.'

'Nice shoes,' said Stan, noticing Torupsun's impeccable brogues. The perforations in the left toe cap depicted a lock; those on his right, a key. 'You got them made?'

'I made them myself. No one fashions keys for me, regardless of their form.' Stan nodded as if this made perfect sense. The shopkeeper was clearly a tad eccentric. 'Is there something I can help you with?'

Stan grimaced apologetically. 'If truth be told, I just came in for a nose. I've got all the keys I need.'

Torupsun smiled. 'Are you sure? Everyone's locked in or out of something.'

'You got me there,' he laughed. The shopkeeper's face was a conundrum that was difficult to age. When he was listening his skin was so smooth he could pass for thirty, an illusion broken the moment he started talking; when his wrinkles deepened and his expression became old and wise. 'Howz this place work then? I've not seen any price tags.'

'Some things are for sale and some are not. But I'm not motivated by profit. What I desired was a place to share and practice my passion. A place to engender conversation and interaction.'

Stan wasn't sure what that meant, but he nodded agreeably. In the ensuing silence, he pointed to a tapestry on the back wall. It depicted a man holding keys. 'Who's that?'

'That's Portunus – the Roman God of Keys. His festival is on August 17th when keys are thrown onto a fire for good luck. I go there every year.'

'What's with the candle underneath?'

'Let's just say we have a relationship.'

'You worship him?'

'Would that be strange?'

'A bit,' he said, chastened by the shopkeeper's offended tone. 'It's just I didn't think anyone was into those old gods anymore.'

'Oh, you'd be surprised. You can still find devotees of Portunus if you know where to look.'

'Shows how much I know. Never heard of him till now.' He smiled and angled toward the door. 'Well thanks, it's been interesting.'

'Did you know most people are unable to say how many keys they have in their pocket?' Torupsun said, a playful sparkle in his blue eyes.

'Really?'

'How many do *you* have?'

Stan ran his mind's eye over his bunch. 'Five.'

'Shall we see?'

He dug into his pocket, extracted his keyring and clanked it onto the nearest cabinet.

'You're one too many,' the shopkeeper said, separating them out.

Stan scowled at his keys.

'You look puzzled. There's one you've forgotten about, isn't there? But don't worry. Lots of people carry keys they no longer use. Especially those who move home or change their workplace. Most can't be bothered to take a redundant key off the ring and soon forget about it. And despite it being there every day, dangling from the bunch as they fit one of its neighbours into a lock, they don't see it anymore.' He pointed to a little key between two big ones. 'This one I'd wager.'

'How'd you know?'

'An educated guess,' he said, proceeding to point at the other keys in turn. 'This is obviously your car key. These two, front and back door keys. This one looks like it fits a back gate, and this one a locker.'

'I'm impressed.'

'The one you forgot about looks like it fits a file box or something similar.'

'I'm sure you're right, but I can't place it.'

'Take it off then and throw it away.'

Stan frowned. 'What if I need it?'

'I'll give you five pounds for it.'

'Why would you do that?'

'I have a thing for forgotten keys. And what's more, once I'm in possession of a key, I'm usually able to say what it fits.'

'That's quite a claim.'

'Sell it to me and you'll see.'

Stan hesitated, wondering what he might be getting himself into. The shopkeeper's sales banter was way off the beaten path, but he seemed nice enough. 'Go on then.'

'Okay, but before we make the transaction, I must tell you that selling me a key also gives me the right to use it.' He had taken on a serious tone, stating this as if it were the terms of a blood pact.

'Didn't know there were rules on selling keys.'

'There's always been rules, but most have forgotten them.'

'What if I want it back when you tell me what it fits?'

'I promise to sell it back if you so wish. And for the same price.'

'Alright. Deal.' Stan threaded the little key off his hoop as the shopkeeper leant over his counter and took a fiver from his till. They made the exchange and the shopkeeper placed the key on the side of his index finger and spun it several times with his thumb – an impressive trick that Stan thought would be difficult to reproduce.

'It fits a car roof box,' Torupsun said, using his thumb to bring it to a dead stop.

'That's it!' said Stan. 'Hundred and fifty quid and we only used it a couple of times. Got a crack in the lid and we ended up binning it. But you could probably tell from the key right? A man in your business and all. Clever though.'

'So. Do you want it back? Remember, selling it to me gives me the right to use it.'

'Nah. You keep it. That thing'll be long gone. Probably crushed to the size of a pea and buried in landfill.'

The shopkeeper smiled. 'Very well.'

'What are those weird looking keys in that cabinet?'

'My collection of enchanted keys,' the shopkeeper said, wandering over to point through the glass. 'This one was cursed by a witch and this one's made of elven glass. It fits the manacle that chains Balvorus the snow dragon to Mount Anatark.' His eyes blazed as he made these extraordinary claims, but there was no trace of humour in his face. 'This one opens a portal between worlds and that tiny silver one opens a book of spells. The wooden one with the long teeth opens a door in the ground… A few years from now most keys will be obsolete, replaced by key cards and passwords; iris and fingerprint scanners. These won't. These keys are eternal… My favourite is that rusty one at the back. It reconfigures the Great Pyramid of Giza, but it hasn't been used for over four thousand years. It has a telescopic barrel that reaches a lock set deep in a stone block. It locks the Queen's and King's chambers and opens the Chamber of Knowledge.'

Stan laughed, but the shopkeeper didn't. He was either a veteran of dead pan or he truly believed what he was saying. 'Where's the keyhole?' he asked, feeling suddenly awkward for his outburst.

'I'm not at liberty to dispense such information.'

'Fair enough. Better safe than sorry eh? Won't there be people out there looking for these keys?'

'There are. But they'll not find them.'

'How much would one set me back?'

Torupsun looked horrified. 'These aren't for sale. Display purposes only.'

'Don't you worry about someone stealing them? I noticed you don't have any security.'

'Woe betide anyone who steals from me,' the shopkeeper said, face hardening and voice dropping an octave. Stan was taken aback and was instantly reminded of a scene in Lord of the Rings where Bilbo accuses Gandalf of wanting the One Ring for himself. The wizard had responded with a display of power that scared the shit out of the little hobbit: the room darkening and the roof beams creaking. There was no supernatural activity going on here, but Torupsun's sudden change in demeanour was a good match. 'There have been thefts,' he said, continuing in a brighter, almost cheery tone, 'but I always get them back.' He walked to an adjacent cabinet and gestured to its contents. 'If you're looking to purchase a key with a bit of history, you might be interested in these.'

Stan went over to look. The cabinet's keys were a motley bunch. Some were little more than rusty bits of iron; but there were some stylish and elegant ones with beautifully crafted handles. They were all price tagged, varying from fifty to five hundred pounds. 'So what do these fit?'

'The provenance of each key is documented here,' Torupsun said, slipping a book out from under the cabinet, 'but I'll be happy to give you a little tour. Number three is from the jewellery box of Catherine the Great. Nine's from Al Capone's cell in Alcatraz and eleven's from the Indomitable Spirit's secret cell in the bowels of the Caliste. Twelve fitted a padlock on Winston Churchill's shed and Nineteen once unlocked Shakespeare's front door.'

Stan had mentally shrugged off Torupsun's harmless collection of enchanted keys, but these had price tags. Sooner or later some poor sucker was going to believe what was written in Torupsun's book and shell out some serious money for a piece of junk. 'Really,' he said a little too harshly. 'I mean, how can you be sure?'

'You'll just have to take my word for it,' the shopkeeper replied. 'The value of anything is based on its perceived worth. Which is why an art collector will pay a fortune for a forgery. Taking pride in ownership until the very second it's revealed as a fake. After that they can barely look at it. The painting hasn't changed — just their perception of it. If you believe in the provenance of these keys, you'll find my prices fair.'

Stan straightened up, realising the shopkeeper's whole line of banter was just an elaborate sales technique. Getting him talking and imbuing a sense of debt. He'd sold Torupsun a useless key for a fiver and had taken up so much of his time that without a purchase, it would be difficult to extricate himself without feeling awkward and embarrassed. This cabinet was the pressure sell: a display of keys that ranged in price – each purchase no doubt replaced by another of similar value. Very clever. 'Right then, thanks for your time. I'll no doubt be back at some point.'

He started for the door, but the shopkeeper called after him. 'Are you aware of my key cutting service?'

'No,' he replied turning back. 'But I'll bear it in mind.'

'I offer a unique side-line.'

'And what's that?'

'I cut keys to abstract locks.'

'What's an abstract lock?' Stan asked, interest piqued.

The shopkeeper closed the distance. 'You must have heard of people being awarded the keys to a city and self-help authors claiming the keys to success within their pages. And what about those young men who seek the key to a pretty girl's heart? Think about the brilliant sports coach who unlocks a player's athletic potential or an inspiring teacher who unlocks a student's intellect. All are abstract concepts postulating locks and keys... Think now of an epiphany – that moment of realisation in which your mind opens to something new. Doesn't that feel like a sudden unlocking of something in your head? As if a ghostly key has turned in a mental door, allowing it to swing open?

'Even a simple string of words can function as a key when spoken in the right order and at the right time. Think of the ease with which a good politician or councillor unlocks you to new ways of thinking and how bad ones keep you locked out. Human affairs are peppered with abstract locks and your life is a never-ending hunt for the keys. You understand?'

'I think so. But you said you cut keys to abstract locks. That's impossible.'

'Is it?' Torupsun said, eyes sparkling.

This guy thought Stan, *what an absolute character.* He was gonna have to send some of his mates down here. Would be kind of funny if one of them got hoodwinked into buying Shakespeare's front door key. 'You sell many of these keys?'

'Many over the years. But I don't offer them to anyone. You came during a quiet period when I have the necessary time to craft one. Why don't you give it a go? It'll only take a couple of minutes.'

'How much?' he asked. He had been determined not to be suckered into spending any money, but he was suddenly curious as to how the shopkeeper would cut such a key.

'Ten pounds.'

'Alright then,' he said. He was five pounds up from selling his old roof box key, so he would only be spending a fiver.

'Excellent,' said Torupsun, rubbing his hands together. 'Choose a blank from that rack and think of something you want to unlock.'

Stan spun the rack and found one with an interesting hexagonal bow. 'This'll do.'

'Thought of something?'

'You mentioned athletic potential, how about that? Been trying to break 20 mins on my Parkrun and a little help wouldn't go amiss.'

'Okay. But I'll have to stare at you while I cut it.'

'Bit weird.'

'I imagine so. But abstract keys open warded locks. Do you know of such locks?' Stan shook his head. 'A warded lock contains obstacles called wards that prevent an intruding key from turning. Keys are cut so they can pass those wards. The wards to your athletic potential are physiological and psychological and I need to get a feel of them.'

Stan kept a neutral face as this nonsense streamed through his sceptical mind. But he had no desire to challenge him. The man's eccentricity was endearing, and he had made him feel so welcome. Most shopkeepers wouldn't give you the time of day.

'Okay, I'll just take a browse if it's alright with you.'

As the shopkeeper's machine fired up and began to whir, Stan wandered up another aisle and stopped to look in a cabinet displaying aerial photos of Kofun: Japanese megalithic tombs constructed between the 3rd and seventh century. The aerial shots showed surrounding fields and buildings, giving a sense of the size of the structures - which in some cases were over four hundred meters long and fifty wide. The tombs were huge and from the air they took on the shape of depthless keyholes. He visualised a key big enough to open such a lock and imagined the hand of God reaching down through the clouds and turning it in the hole; an almighty click reverberating through the earth as a new age is suddenly unlocked. He was still staring at the pictures when the whirring wound down and a deep quiet reclaimed the shop.

'All done,' Torupsun said and as Stan went over he performed his trick again, spinning the freshly cut key on his finger and stopping it dead with his thumb. 'That's just ten pounds.'

'That's quite a trick,' said Stan, taking the key and attempting to reproduce it. It was an instant fail and he flicked it straight onto the floor. 'I'll have to practice that one,' he said, bending to pick it up.

'You can return any key I cut for you and I'll give you half of what you paid,' Torupsun said. 'There's no need for a receipt because I recognise my keys.'

Stan wasn't sure why the shopkeeper would make such a promise, but he thanked him anyway and pocketed the key. 'Howz it work then?' he asked, still not sure if the shopkeeper was taking the piss or if this was his way of selling novelty keys. Service with a show – a way to make more sales and justify his prices.

'The lock will present itself when you need it,' he replied with a clergyman's confidence.

'Right. I'll see you then.'

He left the shop and its oddball proprietor and was glad to be out in the air of sanity.

That Saturday morning, he pulled into the car park at Sewerby Hall. He didn't like to run with his wallet and phone in his shorts, so he hid them in the glove compartment and locked up. He jogged up to the start line where the runners were milling - chatting, warming up and stretching. There wasn't much time left so he made his way to the front as the Master of Ceremonies took to the steps and began his preamble about course safety then read out the names of the latest runners to reach various milestones. As laughter and applause sounded around him, Stan slid his hand into his pocket and felt around his key ring for his latest addition. As his fingers closed on the bow his hand pushed deeper into his pocket and his wrist twisted as if he was turning it in a lock. An involuntary and unexpected movement that was met with a strange resistance - generating a tremor that ran through him from top to toe. He had no time to dwell on the sensation because the starter's countdown ended and he surged forward with the other runners, round the first corner and onto the headland towards Bridlington.

He didn't feel any different and he soon forgot about the key, his full concentration on the run as he reeled in runner after runner. He breezed through the woods near the end and crossed the finish line with energy to spare. He was promptly issued with a tab that said 11th place – which didn't mean much with respect to time. It all depended who was there and how many showed up. Barcode scanned and t-shirt soaked, he trudged back to his car and drove home. He opened his laptop at 12.30 and checked the website for the latest results. His name was there, his time 19.42; over 30 seconds improvement on his P.B.

The next week, he went to the bakery again and waited outside until the queue died down. When the last customer left, he went in and stepped up to the counter where Lizzy was busy arranging cake trays.

'Can I help?' she said, straightening with a smile.

As he opened his mouth an older woman walked out from the back. 'I'll take over Lizzy, you go for your break... What can I get you sir?'

'A chocolate flapjack,' he said, maintaining his smile despite monumental disappointment. His eyes snatching a last glimpse of Lizzy as she slipped away.

As he walked down the street, munching away, he reflected on the fact he was now thinking of Lizzy whenever he saw chocolate flapjack – an association he decided to keep to himself if he was ever lucky enough to date her. Which from the way it was going, might be never.

On the way home he stopped by the key shop. He was keen to report back to the proprietor who he found locking the lid of a new display.

'Morning. What's that?'

'It an article on The Ceremony of Keys,' said Torupsun, turning to him with a smile. 'Performed every night at The Tower of London for the past 700 years. At 21:52 to be precise. It's carried out by Yeomen Warders – the chief of which carries a candle lantern and the Queens keys. It's a gate closing ritual, historically to secure the residents of the Tower, but more recently the Crown Jewels.'

'Portunus'll be impressed.'

'I beg your pardon?'

'That key god,' Stan replied, nodding to the tapestry on the back wall. 'He's gotta be impressed with that – respecting the keys and all.'

'I expect he is.'

'Interesting isn't it?' he said, looking around at the panoply of keys.

'What is?'

'All this key stuff.'

Torupsun looked around as if seeing his collection for the first time. 'What interests me is not the locks and keys themselves, but the use they're put to. This collection is naught but hunks of metal; my interest analogous to that a carpenter takes in the contents of his toolbox. A good carpenter buys the best quality chisels and keeps them sharp – but his primary passion is what he creates with them. Granted, I have no say in how people use their locks and keys, but it is that which fascinates me. What people wish to secure and what they desire to set free. Where someone places a lock tells you a lot about their values and insecurities. Their secrets and weaknesses. People put locks on doors and cupboards, but also cages, safes and chastity belts... Try to think of someone who possesses no keys and without recourse to the homeless or ascetic gurus, you'll struggle. Most people have several keys, abstract and tangible, and those with many tend to be those with greater wealth and influence... Only those without keys can be truly free.'

Stan tipped his head to the rows of cabinets. 'What does all this say about you then?'

The shopkeeper smiled. 'You're right - a lot could be learned about me through a careful study of these cabinets. But would anyone know what to look for?'

'I guess not.'

'Answer me this: Why do people use locks?'

'Like you said, to keep things secure.'

'No. They use them because *others* exist. In a world without others, you wouldn't need them. Locks were born out of human concepts of fear, retribution and greed. Without *others*, such concepts are meaningless.'

'I suppose.'

'I expect you're here to report back on that key. Did it work?'

'New PB and quite easily too. So I guess it did.'

'Are you pleased?'

'Yeah, course.'

'Even though the project was outsourced to a key.'

'I still ran it didn't I?'

'But you said it was easy. Isn't it the blood sweat and tears of a pursuit that gives satisfaction to its achievement? If the key unlocked your potential, isn't that cheating?'

Stan frowned at this unexpected line of questioning. '*You* sold me it. Aren't you supposed to be bigging it up?'

'Oh, the key performed as I expected. I'm interested in how you rationalise the achievement. If *achievement* is the right word.'

'Well it doesn't bother me. I'm getting on a bit and any help's welcome. And look... No offence, but I've been reading up on this type of thing. Sportsmen use lucky charms and rituals all the time and it's their belief in them that helps.'

'Did you have belief in the key whilst you were running your race?'

'No... But there must have been something subconscious going on.'

Torupsun grinned. 'There are millions of biological locks in the human body – receptors on cells activated by agonist molecules such as hormones and neurotransmitters. These molecular keys cause effects in the cells that can manifest as joy, pain, stress and increased performance. But these locks can be fooled by artificial keys. Morphine mimics the shape of natural endorphin keys. THC in cannabis unlocks cannabinoid receptors and LSD the 5HT2A receptor. Depending on the dose, these artificial keys can cause effects more powerful than what you can generate naturally... Last week I cut you an abstract skeleton key that tricked all those physiological and psychological locks that were preventing you from achieving your athletic potential.'

Stan laughed at both the absurdity of the idea and the unexpected detour into complex biology. 'Like a steroid then?'

'Like a steroid,' Torupsun agreed, 'but without the side effects. My keys are more discerning.'

Stan smiled through a scrunched-up face. 'I'm afraid I'm not buying it. We'll just have to agree to disagree.'

'You admit it worked though?'

'In a fashion.'

'Then why not try another key?'

'I don't know about that.'

'Are you sure? I can cut a key to benefit any aspect of your life.'

Stan was posturing to leave, but the shopkeeper's words held him there. He looked out through the window in a moment of indecision then back at the shopkeeper. 'Okay, why not? It'll be a test. If the next key works, I'll have to think a bit deeper about it. What have I got to lose?'

'What *have* you got to lose?' Torupsun said, studying him with blowtorch eyes before taking up position behind his counter. 'What do you want this time?'

'How about a key that'll make me sharper at work?'

'What do you do for a living?'

'I'm a car salesman. But not a great one. This guy Marcus I work with – he's on a whole different level. Three sales to every one of mine. He's got all his figures memorized and never misses a beat. Charms the underwear off the ladies and has the tough guys laughing as they hand him their credit cards. I wanna be like him... Better if possible.'

'A key to your intellect then?'

'That'll do.'

'Very well, but you've got to ask for it – give me permission to cut it.'

'A key to my intellect please,' he said, feeling more than a little foolish. 'Is it ten pounds again?'

'I'm afraid that was an introductory offer. This one will cost you fifty.'

'Fifty quid! You're kidding?'

'What's fifty pounds against all the extra commission you'll make?'

'That's if it *works!*'

'If it doesn't, I'll give you a full refund. I'll even write so much on your receipt.'

Stan shook his head, wishing he'd walked out. 'I'm not carrying that sort of wedge.'

'I take cards. Despite their vulgarity, I've kept up with modern developments.'

'A full refund if it doesn't work? No questions asked?'

'No questions asked.'

'Go one then... You should get a job in our garage. You'd put Markus to shame.'

Stan produced his card, made the transaction and selected another blank. Then he turned away to browse the cabinets as the shopkeeper started cutting – his speculative gaze burning a hole in his back.

A week later Stan was back in the shop again. He thought about what would happen if he told Torupsun the second key hadn't worked and asked for a refund. But it *had* worked. First thing Monday morning he'd sat down at his desk and with his hand in his pocket, slipped his new key into another invisible lock. After that business had been great.

When the shopkeeper asked him how it had gone, he decided to come clean. 'It worked a treat. Put that Markus kid to shame. I knew just what to say and made all the right moves. If I can keep it up till the end of the month, I'll be on for the company sales record.'

'You don't feel bad the key was doing the work?'

'Nah. I still think it's psychological. But even if your theory's true, it's no different to necking some black coffee or taking a nip of whisky.'

'What about this Marcus character? Won't your increased commission result in a decrease in his? Hasn't the turning of that key deprived him? Stolen from him?'

Stan grinned. 'You sure know how to promote your wares. No. Markus has his own customers and I'm not poaching from him.'

'Did Marcus have a good week?'

'Not one of his best.'

'Could it be that your increase in charm funnelled his customers over to you?'

'Okay – you got me. But he's been getting the lion's share of the punters the whole time I've been there.'

'If you found out he'd been using a similar key, what would you think?'

Stan felt like a lone king in a game of chess - chased into a corner by a pair of rooks. 'Alright, I get what you're saying. But come on. This key thing's only a bit of fun and everything'll settle down next week. It's only fair I get some glory. Marcus is a natural salesman. He won the gene lottery and that's not fair on the rest of us.'

The shopkeeper nodded. 'Interesting rationalisation.'

'It's the truth.'

'Would you like me to cut you another key?'

'No thanks. I can see this becoming a problem for me – though I still reckon it's just a bit of positive thinking. Life's good right now. Fitness is coming on and work's a breeze.'

'Do you have a young lady to share your good fortune with?'

He thought instantly of Lizzy. 'No.'

The shopkeeper raised his eyebrows. 'But there's someone you've got your eye on?'

'How did you know?'

'It's all over your face.'

'That obvious eh?'

'What if I were to cut you a key to that young lady's heart?'

'You can do that?'

'I can – but it'll cost you a hundred pounds. A key to someone's heart requires the most delicate fashioning.'

'That's going too far,' Stan said, shaking his head. 'A novelty key'll never work for something like that?'

'Because your lucky charm/positive thinking theory won't stretch to it?'

'Yeah, I suppose. Belief in yourself can only go so far. She's either gonna like me or she isn't and what I'm packing on my keyring won't make any difference.'

'What better test of my skills then? If it doesn't work, I'll give you a full refund and I'll have to concede my abstract keys don't work.'

Stan sucked in his lower lip and thought about declining. He didn't really know Lizzy and getting a key cut to her heart felt devious. Something he might later be ashamed of. But he was interested to see what would happen – especially if there was the slightest chance his previous successes could be replicated with her. He could give the key a quick whirl in the shop then get rid of it. If she went out on a date with him, it would be his own work from then on. 'Okay then.'

'Excellent! Pick one of those dainty keys with the ornate tab – one that suits her.'

He spun the rack and was drawn to a brass one with a pair of overlapping hearts on the bow. 'This one.'

'Very good,' said Torupsun. 'As she's not here, you'll have to tell me about her. Can you do that?'

He looked around. 'That's worse than staring at me... Go on then. But if someone comes in you'll have to stop.'

'That's easily solved,' said the shopkeeper, strolling over to lock the door and turning his sign to closed. He returned to the counter and fired up his cutter. 'Ready when you are.'

'Her name's Lizzy and she works in the bakery where I buy flapjack.'

The shopkeeper looked up. 'That's not what I need. Tell me why you like her and *mean* it.'

Awkward thought Stan, but he couldn't back out now. 'She's petite. Has this mop of wavy red hair under her hair net; tied back with a ribbon... She's got this way of moving that's like a ballet dancer. The way she weaves around the other staff and goes on her tiptoes to take something off a shelf. Like she's made of polystyrene. Her laugh's odd – squeaky, but infectious. There's a tattoo of a rose on the inside of her wrist and you can just see it when she reaches behind the hygiene glass and her sleeve rides up... She sounds kind – the way she speaks to the old dears in the queue...'

'Nearly there – something more.'

'She blushes really bad when she gets flustered.'

'Okay done,' the shopkeeper said, turning off his machine and handing him the key. As the motor whirred down, Stan held it up to the light. It suited her perfectly and he imagined turning it in her chest – a gentle click preceding her embarrassed blush. A ludicrous but exciting idea.

'Well thanks. Fingers crossed eh?'

'Before you go, I want you to know you can return your keys at any time for half what you paid. I collect those with stories. But I must have the full set.'

'I'll bear that in mind,' said Stan and left, thinking of Lizzy and his double hearted key.

The next day he took his new key to the bakery, holding it in his pocket as he shuffled to the counter. And just like at his desk at work and on the start line for Parkrun, an involuntary twitch pushed it deeper into his pocket and turned his wrist. *Click.*

'Can I help?' Lizzy asked.

'A chocolate flapjack please,' he replied, with what he hoped was a charming smile. She smiled back and reached behind the hygiene glass to fish one out. 'I saw the Cherries poster in the window, you into them?'

'Yeah, big time,' she said, straightening up. 'It was me who put it up.' She twisted his flapjack in paper and placed it on the counter. 'That's 65 pence please.'

'I might see you at the Cherries gig on Saturday then.'

'You might,' she replied, a wry smile on her rapidly flushing face. Stan blushed in response, realising he had become more than a faceless customer. He left with his heart beating out of his chest and didn't look back. The exchange had vanquished his appetite and it wasn't until three days later that he discovered his chocolate flapjack, squished and melted in his inside pocket.

Lizzy was at the Cherries gig on Saturday, sitting with her friends at a table near the door. And by the way she flew over, it was like she had been waiting for him all night. Within minutes they were talking like old friends and within hours they were an item – mouths locked together in a dark corner as the band they'd come to see ran through their tracks unheard.

They'd been dating over a month when Stan decided to take Torupsun's keys off his bunch and hang them behind the backdoor. The idea that the most recent addition had unlocked Lizzy's heart was ridiculous, but it was starting to gnaw at him. He needed proof the shopkeeper's theories were all nonsense and that his relationship was based on natural attraction, rather than some magical slavery to a key. And to his relief nothing happened. Lizzy continued to dote on him, he continued to outperform Markus and his Parkrun times steadily improved. Life was good and a month later he decided he didn't want the keys in the house anymore. He took them out to the bin, but as he flipped the lid, he remembered the shopkeeper's offer. Half back on all keys with no questions asked. He made a quick calculation. Eighty pounds. With all his extra commission, he was in for a good wage at the end of the month. But that was over a week away and he was about spent up. Eighty quid would be enough to take Lizzy out on Saturday night. Perhaps to that great tapas restaurant on Blands Cliff. So he put the keys in his pocket and set off into town.

When he arrived, the shopkeeper was bent over an open cabinet arranging a collection of ancient padlocks. He welcomed him with a smile and paid out just as he had promised – as if he had been expecting the keys back all along. They exchanged pleasantries, but before they could get into their usual key talk, the door opened and another customer stepped in. He didn't want to hang around, so he bade Torupsun farewell and went home.

Over the next few weeks, Lizzy became distant and moody, staring into space all the time as if imagining somewhere she'd rather be. When he asked what was wrong, she blamed work. But he wasn't convinced. Their kisses began to feel one sided and she became tense whenever he touched her. He began to suspect the worst until one day she confronted him in the hallway – telling him she'd met someone else before turning her back and walking out.

His heartbreak was immense and he wracked his brains for days, trying to understand what had gone wrong. They hadn't fallen out or rowed. Barely had any disagreements in their whole time going out. His thoughts inevitably circled in on the key Torupsun cut to her heart and for a short while he entertained the idea that it really worked and that their breakup had something to do with him selling it back. But he soon decided he was clutching at straws. If the keys had any real power, his work and running would also have been affected. But he was still doing well with both. No, Lizzy had left him for non-magical reasons, but he was mystified as to what they were.

A few days later he went to the bakery, hoping to catch her on her break. Just to talk. To get a handle on what went wrong. He looked through the window several times during the morning and saw no sign of her. A week later, he saw her coming towards him on Queen Street. He braced for a confrontation, but she ducked into the key shop without seeing him. He picked up his pace and followed her in, just in time to see her kiss Torupsun full on the lips before disappearing through the rear door.

'*You're* Lizzy's new fella!' Stan bawled, storming over to the counter. 'It's that key isn't it?'

'You sold me it of your own free will – giving me the right to whatever it unlocks.'

'You bastard. You can't do this?'

'Can't I?' the shopkeeper replied, gesturing to the door through which she'd disappeared.

'I'll report you?'

Torupsun laughed. 'To whom? And say what? That I enslaved your girlfriend with a magic key? A key you used to the same end?'

This was too much for Stan and his spiralling temper exploded like a geyser. He charged around the counter in a red mist, resolved to lay him out. He didn't see the shopkeeper pull a key out from behind the counter and fit it into the air. As Stan cocked his arm, Torupsun turned the key and his ensuing punch was inaccurate and lame, missing him completely. He tried another, but his strength had deserted him and he tripped over his own feet to fall against the counter. The shopkeeper placed the heel of his key-hole brogue against his shoulder and pushed him to the ground.

'Remember this?' Torupsun said, indicating the floating key. 'It's the key to your athleticism.' He produced a second key, fitting it to another invisible lock beside the first. 'And what about this one? The key to your intellect.' He turned this key a quarter turn and Stan felt a seismic shift in his head.

'I'll...get...you Mr Shopkeeper Man,' was all he could say, his mind a gloopy stew and his muscles, uncoordinated and weak.

As he rose the shopkeeper's pupils changed: the left morphing into the shape of a lock; the right, that of a key. Enlarging to the extent they crossed the border of his iris' and into the whites of his eyes. 'You knew how the keys worked and yet you sold them to me – giving a stranger complete control of your athleticism and intellect. Best of all that sweet girl's heart.' His voice had dropped in pitch again and Stan was once more put in mind of that scene in Lord of the Rings. Only this time the similarities were stronger. As the shopkeeper spoke the room darkened at its periphery, the walls and ceiling creaking as if they were about to implode under some invisible strain. 'Go now and never come back,' Torupsun went on, his unworldly baritone causing Stan to cower. 'I don't want you upsetting Lizzy. Speak a word of this to anyone and I'll turn these keys all the way and you'll spend the rest of your life as a cripple and a halfwit... Go on, get out of my shop... If you behave, I'll turn them back some.'

Stan rose in knee-trembling fear and staggered out like a drunkard, unable to truly comprehend what was going on. Outside, he leant on a lamppost to steady himself. When his strength and co-ordination came back, he looked back through the window to find the shopkeeper staring out, hands operating the floating keys and making fine adjustments. His mental faculties came back and his predicament crystalized. He had been played by a demon in the shape of a man. And now some of the letters on the shop front were disappearing, leaving only those of the shopkeeper's name. Then these lifted free, scrambling in the air to reset themselves – *Torupsun* morphing into *Portunus*. Stan gasped. Not a demon, but the Roman God of Keys. As he stared through the window Portunus gave him a dismissive wave and reached for the floating keys. It was a terrifying threat and Stan lurched away, scattering shoppers with his wild eyes.

The Shadow King

To begin, it's probably best if I just state my situation simply and expand on the details. My name is Andrew Jons, I have a beautiful wife Josie and two wonderful children, Stevie and Maddie. I haven't seen them for the last five years because I've been living in a weird version of Scarborough in which all living things have been removed. Their shadows are still cast though - waxing and waning as if they were still here.

My arrival here was a swift descent into near madness. I woke late, opening my eyes to an alarm clock that had failed its duty – the 8.35 on its display informing me I was already late for work. I turned to shake Josie and was surprised to find a cold space where she should have been. I leapt up and stormed onto the landing to call her, angry she'd let me sleep in. When there was no answer, I went back to the bedroom cursing; meaning to ring work, but unable to find my phone. I usually plug it in at the side of the bed, but there was only its white charging cable - lying on the floor in a redundant coil.

I checked the kids' rooms and discovering their beds vacant, dressed and hurried downstairs. Coats and bags were missing from the pegs and three Weetabix-encrusted bowls were stacked in the sink. I wracked my brains, trying to remember if Josie had said anything about a change of plan – perhaps a school trip she was taking the kids in early for. She often tells me important stuff while I'm watching telly and I usually grunt my understanding without ever taking my eyes off the screen. The information goes in, but it's uploaded with the mental equivalent of a disappearing-ink pen, and it's gone in few seconds. Sooner, if there's a glass of wine in my hand. So, when nothing came to mind, I assumed that's what happened. I went to the landline to ring work, but there was no dialling tone. Thinking someone had yanked the connection from the wall, I pulled the sofa out to check it. And it was while I was squatting down that I noticed how quiet it was.

There's a bowling green near our house that's surrounded by trees and every morning you can hear a chorus of chattering birds on a background of road noise. Sounds I now realised were gone. I opened the front door and listened, straining my ears to pick up anything beyond the gentle stirring of leaves – a sound I rarely used to notice and one that was to become perpetually prominent in my new life. Unsettled, I walked the path and opened the gate. Several abandoned cars were positioned in the road and one was parked with its door open. Not a soul to be seen or heard.

I got an urge to call out a pathetic hello - as if the street was private property I needed permission to enter. But when I saw a delivery truck pulled up on the pavement, I ran to that instead. The back shutter was raised and its load of cardboard boxes was in full view. I looked around, hoping to see the driver, but saw a shadow instead. Coming at me along the path.

It was a bright June day and shadows were sharp. I looked up, because it's what you do when you see a shadow that's not attached to a subject – the only sane interpretation, that it's being cast by something airborne. But there was nothing up there but clear blue sky. The shadow passed under me and I spun to follow it, spotting two more coming at me from across the road. Slower this time. On closer inspection, they appeared to be the disembodied shadows of people and they disappeared under a parked car, to re-emerge on the other side. That's right - disappeared underneath without projecting onto the car. Now, I don't know if you've ever been in a situation where reality doesn't conform to your expectation, but for me it was the mental equivalent of sleeping on my arm – my head suddenly fizzy and numb. And when my faculties returned, instead of pins and needles, there was this feeling of cold watery dread.

Heart rate soaring, I ran to the local shop and through its open door. It should have been busy with schoolkids, but the place was empty. The till draw was open and a there was a pack of bacon on the counter. I called through to the back, only then seeing the weak shadows generated by the overhead lighting, moving and milling around me. With a panicky tunnel vision, I ran for my kids' school, suddenly desperate to see them. I passed an empty pram on a street corner and several open doors - one with a key ring dangling from the lock. I called out - not caring to look stupid anymore. But all I got in return was my own frantic voice, echoed back from deserted terraces.

I burst into Gladstone Road School's empty reception, rattling a security door that prevented further passage – one that could only be opened by a buzzer behind the receptionist's desk. I called through the window several times, but soon lost patience and climbed through. I rushed along the corridor, calling out with increasing hysteria, looking into classrooms that were every bit as you'd expect them to be, except for the missing pupils and the graveyard silence. Chairs were pulled out from tables strewn with books and stationary. Work was written on white boards – some of it incomplete and ending mid-sentence.

Maddie's coat was hanging on her peg outside her classroom. One she had personalised with a frog sticker. I burst in without knocking and stared at the shadows of absent children sitting at their desks and their teacher's larger one, pacing up front. At that point I became overwhelmed by a nauseating disorientation and was sick – barely making it to the little sink the kids use to clean up after art lessons. I ran from school with a spinning head, telling myself it was all a lucid dream and that I'd soon wake up. I jumped the railings at the rear of the playground and ran into a lifeless Sainsbury's where dozens of part-filled trolleys were abandoned in the aisles. Checkouts were loaded with items; hot meats sweltered on the rotisserie counter and foreign money fluttered on the bureau-de-change. Shadows milling everywhere, but still no one to be seen.

That's when the day turned into a blur, because I went straight to the drinks aisle and grabbed the first bottle I came to. Bacardi I think it was, and chugged half its contents in three desperate gulps. Cowardly, I know, but dream or no dream, a spiralling panic was taking hold and it was the only action I thought would stop it. Intoxicated, I half ran, half staggered into town, ending up at the accountants where Josie works. That's all I remember of that first day and I woke next morning on one of the green leather sofas in reception. That day went much the same way, as did that first week – a kind of pissed-up confusion during which I walked the streets, shouting at the sky. Imploring this strange world to tell me what it wanted and begging it to set me free.

In time, I settled into my new existence – sobering up and trying to make sense of it all. In the early days, I spent most of the time following my shadow family around the house, trying to identify them and what they were doing. Sometimes I'd talk to them as if they were still there - sad monologues in which I'd tell them about my day and ask questions they never answered. When they left the house, I tried to follow - soon giving up after discovering it was nigh on impossible. It was alright if they were on their own, but as soon as they entered a crowded area, their shadows got mixed up with everyone else's. And if it was cloudy – it was a total non-starter.

I kiss Josie's shadow every morning and night – whether its cast by her night lamp or the natural light from the window. Telling her I love her and that we'll soon be together again. I watch when she reads the kids a bedtime story, tying to imagine how they're positioned and what they're saying. And when she goes downstairs, I read them another story – hoping it reaches them in their dreams. They've kept the tradition of watching a film on Saturday night and I often sit with them, watching one of my films while they watch theirs. Imagining we're all sat there together. A new Disney film was on the dining room table when I woke up one day and I knew they'd be watching it that night. So, when their shadows gathered in the front room that evening I watched it with them. It was a sad one and I cried, as much for myself as for the old man in the film. Just sat there on the sofa between two members of my shadow family, blubbering my eyes out.

In summer I often crack a beer in the garden and watch Stevie's shadow moving around the trampoline – trying to imagine his airborne contortions. We used to play a game called *The Moves* in which I invented elaborate ways of knocking him over or tossing him in the air. Giving names to those that were any good. There was the *Rolling Pin, The Flip, Tickle and Slide, The Rhino Charge* and *The Gyroscope,* to name but a few. A game I enjoyed as much as he did. Moves only possible due to my relative size and superior strength. It's been five years since we last played and even if I could magically realign with his world, he'd probably be too heavy to throw around. I remember the last time we played, and it was only a quick ten minutes, the end of which he begged me to go on. 'One more Daddy,' he called after me, in a squeaky voice I'm beginning to forget. 'One more *pleeeaase!*' I placated him with a promise to play later – a promise I meant to keep, but for whatever reason never did.

I often think about my last night at home. I spent some quality time with Stevie, playing with his soldiers before putting him to bed. There was tickling and laughing and a made-up story about Croccy the Crocodile – an elaboration on a character I used to play at the pool, swimming underwater and pulling him down. As good a farewell as I could have mustered, even if I had known what was to become of me.

But with Maddie and Josie it was different. The last time I saw my little girl she was bent over a drawing, coloured felt tips laid out in a neat line, hair hanging over her face. I stuck my head into her room and told her to pack up for bed. It's a cruel truth that in most cases you never know when you're seeing someone for the last time. I deeply regret not going in now – to praise her picture and ask after her day. Instead, I left Josie to do her bedtime story and went downstairs to pour a glass of wine, not knowing the time left with my family was running away like sand in an hourglass. Josie went to bed early to read and was asleep when I went in. I can't remember what film I stayed up to watch and I don't care. But I'd give anything to go back and praise Maddie's picture and go to bed early to make love to my wife.

A week after I arrived here, laminated photos of me began to appear, zip-tied to lampposts or blue-tacked to shop windows. The photo was one I remembered, taken in the woods during a long walk with the kids. *Missing*, it said beneath my mugshot with Josie's mobile number in bold. It's an odd feeling to see a picture of yourself in that context and kind of ironic given that from my perspective everyone's missing but me.

That first Christmas I found a note under Maddie's pillow, addressed to Father Christmas:

Forget the presents. Bring Daddy back and I'll never ask for anything ever again. Cross my heart and hope to die.

Three lines of an eight-year old's scrawl and it was like a punch to the breastbone that kept going, dropping me into a heap on her bed. My family can't possibly know what happened to me, but I hope they don't think I deserted them.

From the photos that appear in our albums, it looks like Maddie's gonna be tall and Stevie's turning into a little bruiser. Josie was sporting a new haircut on her most recent picture and I'm dreading the day I see one of her with another man. Not that I'd blame her. I can't expect her to wait forever - especially for a husband who's disappeared off the face of the earth. I often look beyond her smile for clues to her happiness – wondering if she still thinks of me and how long it'll be before she moves on.

For the first few months, I could only guess what they'd been up to. But then I remembered a parent's evening during which Maddie's teacher said she gets the class to write up what they've done at weekends. So now, I've taken to going into school every Monday – my little girl the author of a weekly column I can't wait to get my hands on. And thank God she loves to write. The piece is always titled The Weekend Report and she usually fills a couple of pages of an orange exercise book. The report's never as detailed as I'd like though. Of course it isn't. She writes from a child's perspective and Stevie only gets a mention if he's done something annoying. Her last report detailed the jam tarts she made with her mum and the ginger cat that jumped over our fence and scared birds from the feeder. I try to fill in the gaps about Stevie by looking through *his* schoolwork. But his writing about home is sparse and when it appears, tends to focus on action figures and TV shows. He did mention he's learnt to backflip though and now when I watch his shadow on the trampoline, I can tell when he does one.

Last week a For Sale sign appeared in our garden – the worst news I've had by far. I panicked big style – knowing if I didn't find out where they were moving to, I would lose them forever. I searched the house, found some property brochures in Josie's bedside drawers and went to check them out - trying to guess which ones she'd be interested in. Without my income, it must be hard to stay on top of the bills and I wondered if she was being forced to downsize. But I checked her paper statements and she seemed to be managing. Looks like she's shopping at Aldi instead of Sainsbury's though and spending only on necessities. If it's not money – it could be she just wants a new start. Totally understandable given the circumstances. We bought this house together and she must be haunted by memories. I know I am. They haven't moved yet – but I'm dreading the day I wake to find their possessions in boxes and a removal van outside.

Anyway... enough self-pity and back to the intricacies of my new life. Every morning, I wake to a new *reset* with all inanimate objects arranged, I believe, as they will be at 12:21 in the real world. There are a few lines of evidence for this. Analogue clocks are frozen on this time, the roads are filled with cars and it appears to be lunchtime everywhere: sandwiches laid out in various states of preparation and fish and chips shop ranges filled with hot fat. Most shadows make sense, but there are occasions when they don't match the physical environment. Sometimes they're incomplete, because the object casting them is in a different reset position, allowing sunlight to reach the missing parts. Other times, it's the other way around and I see shadows within shadows – a reset object now casting a darker shadow over the original one. At 12:21 (unless *I've* been moving things around) all shadows line up perfectly and I get the *glimpse*, where for a single second, I can see and hear the world with all living things back in it. A beautiful, precious moment of HD reality.

The glimpse is my favourite time of day. It's a chance to see Josie and the kids and it gives me hope that one day I'll return to them. If I'm at home, I'll follow one of them around, orientating myself in such a way to optimise my view. It's hit and miss though, as it's difficult to tell which way someone is facing from their shadow. I once glimpsed Maddie blowing her nose and Josie bending to tie her shoelaces – wasted opportunities that got me down. But sometimes I get lucky. I once caught a glimpse of Josie in the garden, hair ruffed up and glowing with captured sunlight. Another time I was in Maddie's classroom and she appeared right in front of me, wearing a plastic pinny with paint all over it and laughing at her friends. And I once got a glimpse of Stevie at nursery, pushing a little red train along a wooden track, his lips pursed and dribbling as he made chu-chu noises.

The glimpse I cherish most was last summer when I woke to find the beach bags gone. I knew there was a good chance they'd gone to Nalgo Bay, to set up on our favourite stretch of sand. I biked out and positioned myself between the sea and the cluster of shadows I hoped was them. When the glimpse came, they were huddled together looking out to sea, towels around their shoulders and sandwiches in hands. The type of picture you'd put on a canvas and mount above your fireplace. It was my favourite glimpse so far and it reduced me to tears. More beautiful than sun glistening on water, and just as painful to look at.

Does my family glimpse me too? The magic lasts for less than a second – long enough to discern movement and to get a reaction. But there's never any widening of eyes or the shocked recoil you'd expect from someone surprised by my appearance. So, no. The glimpse is one way and I'm glad. If I knew they could see me I'd be tempted to stand there with a placard telling them I was trying to get back. A stupid, selfish idea that would only scare them.

So...what do you do when you're trapped in this shadowland?

Get a routine's what you do, if you don't want to go mad. On a typical day I wake naturally between six and eight. There's no point setting the alarm, because it begins the day in its reset configuration, thinking it's already gone off. In the depths of winter, I wake with a frown and the big light shining in my face – Josie no doubt needing it to dress and forgetting to switch it off. Our house can be messy or tidy – the fridge stocked or empty. There might be a new drawing on Maddie's bedroom wall, a new book on Josie's bedside table or a new game on Stevie's PlayStation. On a few rare occasions, I've opened the toilet door to find a poo in the bowl. It's not as offensive as you might imagine though – for as disgusting as it might be it's the closest physically link to my family. I know it's weird, but I can't help looking into the bowl before I flush, trying to guess who made it by its size. I know where that person will be at 12.21 and in which direction they'll be looking. Tempting as it is to be there for the glimpse, I always pass. Their faces are sure to be set in a very private way and it would be wrong. Wouldn't want anyone looking at me when I'm getting behind a stubborn one!

The world moves on day by day. Technology and fashion evolve. I've got running water, electric and gas. The TV plays DVDs, but I can't get any programmes. Computers work, but there's no internet and I can't access picture and video files. There's no newspapers and most books have sections where the words *Censored by the Shadow King* have replaced big chunks of text. More about him later.

There's 24hrs between each reset and a lot can change in the interim. I was once puzzled by the shadows of two men moving up and down the side of a house. I couldn't fathom it until a scaffold appeared the next day. Workmen were painting the second floor and hadn't erected the scaffold until the afternoon. At 12.21 their poles and clamps were in their van and that's where they stayed for the entirety of my day. Over the course of a week the paintwork was sanded down and a new coat of green gloss appeared in the staggered way that characterises the progress of all big changes in my world. And on the last morning, there were shadows of workmen on the wall, climbing an invisible scaffold that had been taken down before the reset.

It's mainly weekends I stay home now, when there's a good chance of my family being around. Weekdays I go exploring – looking for a way out. I don't waste time washing or worrying about what to wear. When there's no one around to see and smell you, those things don't matter anymore. So much of what we do is to impress others, but when you're alone you're driven only by the basic desires of hunger and thirst, warmth and shelter. All else is superfluous vanity. Still brush my teeth though. Poor mouth hygiene isn't something I can tolerate, no matter how long I've been here.

What I desire most is what I used to have: family, friends, laughter and conversation. The three gods I formerly worshiped were my phone, the internet and box sets, and I don't miss any of them now. The only non-essential not to have lost its charm is music. I've got a vinyl collection that so far Josie hasn't thrown out and most day's I'll spin one of my favourite albums. Much of what I listen to is transportive – familiar riffs that allow me to inhabit the energy and hope of another time. And it's an opportunity to hear another voice.

Besides loneliness, the hardest thing to deal with over here is the quiet. When Josie shared a house during her student-nurse days I often stayed over. She had this old fridge in her room that used to hum. A sound you didn't notice until it cut out while you were trying to get to sleep. What you thought was silence was suddenly replaced by a deeper quiet you wouldn't have thought possible – a quiet so vacuous it became even more difficult to sleep. That happens here, but on a much grander scale. When there's no breeze to rustle the leaves, the silence bores through your head – creating a yearning cavity that's difficult to ignore. Those times I go running for my vinyl, or if I'm out - to the seaside and the unending crash of waves and jostle of boats.

When I go out, I mostly cycle. There are three decent mountain bikes on our street and I usually steal one – though in my world stealing's the wrong word. Borrowing's not even right. The bikes are always back with their owners at the next reset and without any damage or wear. I've tried driving, but the roads are so clogged it's impossible to get very far. The exceptions are Christmas Day and New Year Day when most people are having their family dinner and I can get around pretty well, driving on the occasional path and if necessary, abandoning one car for another. Those in the middle of the road have their keys in and always start.

At some point I do a bit of shopping, usually grabbing something to eat on the go. I rarely cook myself, cos what's the point? I'd only be cooking for one and there's so much hand-to-mouth out there. Town has become an all you-can-eat buffet and I often eat straight from shelves without need for cutlery. I change my clothes in the stores, usually because what I'm wearing isn't suited to the weather, rather than out of any sense of fashion. Dressing straight from the hanger and leaving my old stuff on the floor. I dress for comfort these days and rarely look in the mirror. Because, let's face it, mirrors are only there to give you someone else's perspective and like I said earlier, I don't need to consider what anyone else thinks. It's a truly liberating way to shop and when I do get a glimpse of my reflection it makes me smile to think about what people would say about some of my less conventional ensembles.

Occasionally, I'll check out a non-essential store just to see what the shadow people are wasting their money on. Usually it's meaningless objects, destined to end up in one of the charity shops down the road. Pet shops are so weird I don't visit them anymore. They still have that strong animal smell, but the cages are uninhabited, the fish tanks running pumps that ripple empty water. Definitely in my top three creepiest places – along with the hospital and the arcades. Hospitals because of all those shadow patients with drips attached and arcades because of those electronic voices imploring you to place your bets or join a game. I used to love arcades, but those voices take on a different feel when you're on your own. It's like they're speaking directly to me and mocking me. And if I'm close when one fires up, I just about shit my pants.

I try to be back before dark as nights here are spooky. Due to the 12:21 reset the streetlights are nearly always off and the only lights are those that have been left on accidently, or those from cars, presumably turned on during a storm. Away from the arcades the harbour is particularly dark and haunting, all those masts rocking from side to side – the tinny jingle of rigging and flapping of flags. Being out at night is the only time the idea of not being alone fills me with dread, as the shadows that dart across those few bright bits of pavement have an assassin-like quality that puts me on edge. I've tried to stay up to see the reset, but come 11:55 I'm always overcome with tiredness and end up falling to sleep. I've tried exercise, coffee and even a few lines of coke I found on a drug dealer's coffee table. But the result is always the same. This world doesn't want me up after midnight – the magic it weaves for reset, not for my unworthy eyes.

Whatever I do each day is cancelled out the next. If I crash a car or set a house on fire they're fully restored by the time I wake up. The same goes for injuries. I once gashed my leg climbing a fence and the next day it was all better again: smooth as a pole dancer's bum and with no scar in sight. I eat all I want without gaining weight and I don't age. Except for stuck-up hair, the reflection that greets me every morning is unchanged. I once buzzed my hair off with clippers and it was back to its original length the next day. I couldn't help thinking of that old Play-Doh toy that sprouts hair through its skull when you push a plunger up its backside and wondering if mine had grown back the same way.

Anything not in contact with me overnight is lost to the reset and back where it will be in the real world at 12:21. I like to sleep naked and I continued to for the first six months. But one morning, I woke to discover my clothes gone. For whatever reason Josie got rid of them and there wasn't a stitch to fit me in the entire house. I walked into town naked, but it was summer and there was no one around to give a shit. I picked out new clobber from top to bottom – starting with underwear and finishing with a flowered bucket hat. Since then, I sleep with my clothes on – footwear and all, which is proper uncomfortable. I loosen my laces, but not too much, as I'm prone to kicking them off and losing them to the reset. And because my clothes stay on, I did a bit of experimentation, discovering that anything taped to my body overnight is still with me the next morning. Nowadays, I tape a thumb drive to my leg before turning in. On it is a folder containing a list of interesting finds and their locations, my thoughts and theories about why I'm here and this piece of writing, which is keeping me sane.

For a time, I held onto the possibility of finding others and wasted many months trying to draw them out. I've driven a fire engine through town with its blue lights flashing and two-tones blaring. And I've built bonfires on the castle headland and sat by them for hours. Reading books and eating chicken thighs - waiting for someone to show up. There was a time when I took whiteboards from W.H. Smith's and set them up in the high street, marker-pen scrawl informing potential readers I'd be back at five o'clock. There's been no contact so far, so either I'm alone or my fellow captives have a massive dose of shyness. Whatever the truth, I've given up looking. *I've* not been shy and if there's anyone out there, they must know where to find me. Nevertheless, despite the resounding emptiness of this place, I've never been able to shake the feeling someone's watching me, or about to step out of the next doorway. Mannequins are the worst. I occasionally come across one with its back turned and I'm often convinced it's a fellow prisoner who's hoping I mistake them for a store dummy. But I always check - heart racing as I grip its moulded shoulder and turn its plastic face around.

I've tried to leave Scarborough, but I'm restricted to a circular area that's centred on my house and has a radius of about three miles. Getting to the edge of this area is like reaching the boundary in a video game. My feet keep moving, but I make no progress, the ground blurring as I switch into a bizarre and unsettling moonwalk. The same is true whether I'm cycling, driving or piloting a boat. I can throw things over this invisible barrier and watch them land – but can't cross myself. Very strange.

I've been just about everywhere I can go, starting with those places I've always wanted to nosey inside: The Toll House on the Marine Drive, the Town Hall and the turret rooms in the Grand Hotel. I've been inside the clock tower at the train station and the one at Holbeck Putting Green, which required a step ladder to access its trapdoor. The latter was an anti-climax as there was nothing up there but an abandoned bird's nest and a coil of frayed rope.

More interesting are the homes of rich folk, many of which are at the end of long driveways or behind big hedges. At first, I felt uncomfortable snooping around, but it soon wore off. No one's gonna know and anything I do is undone by the reset. I found a house with an original 80s arcade, several with top-end Jacuzzis and home cinemas, and dozens with postcard views over the bay. Water beds and luxury four-posters have occasionally tempted me into staying over but it always feels like I'm abandoning my family for a second time and I'm soon home again, tucked up alongside my shadow wife.

Five years on, the things I see behind closed doors continues to amaze me. I've found several mini cannabis factories and two big ones – one on Valley Road and the other in Scalby. In a flat on Castle Road, I found a suitcase of paper money sitting on a draining board. Mixed denominations all shoved together as if they'd been packed in a hurry. I counted the notes on the kitchen table and there was exactly fifty grand. Worthless to me, so I just left it there – more interested in filling my water bottle from the tap.

I've been in the house of a hoarder who must have kept everything that came into her possession. Rooms stacked to the ceiling with boxes of chatty ornaments and craft material. Newspapers, take-away menus and junk mail still in their plastic sleeves, piled so high they covered the windows and blocked the light. Laundry baskets full of old and broken kitchen equipment and carrier bags full of charity shop clothes. Sundry furniture crammed and stacked into the hall, leaving only a narrow corridor to the kitchen which I had to sidle down. And the stink! The warrens in the junk were a haven for rats and their droppings were everywhere, overhung by an aroma of cat shit and piss. So strong it sent me clambering for fresh air, knocking over an ironing board loaded with unopened Christmas presents.

I found an S&M dungeon in the middle of town with three cages and a sex swing – a rack of canes and whips fixed on a red velvet wall and two racks: one bearing ropes, handcuffs and manacles; the other - harnesses and bespoke saddles, fitted with adjustable and seemingly interchangeable phallic extensions. There was a row of changing rooms in which the *Rules of Eliza's Boudoir* were mounted above clothes hooks. Etched on scrolls and fixed in glass picture frames. Opposite the changing rooms was a huge walk-in wardrobe of capes, gowns, masks and eye-watering stilettoes. All this right below a bustling high street, where people shop for underwear *with* gussets and the only sausages in evidence are those baked in pastry!

Over the years I've learnt to find pleasure in my new life – though afterwards it always feels like sacrilege, given my ongoing absence from family. One of my favourite things is to visit a nightclub, spin tunes in the DJ booth and crank the sound system. Then I either dance or exercise. The benefits of exercise don't carry over though, as I can only ever do forty-eight press ups and hold a plank for 82 seconds. But flushing the blood clears the mind and I always feel better, despite having to wince like a pissed-up clubber when I step back out into the daylight. Other times I go to the Indoor Swimming Pool, as there's nothing like doing lengths all on your lonesome. But without lifeguards to fish me out, there's always this nagging fear of drowning. I don't use the changing rooms anymore as I've taken to stripping off in the gallery and jumping in from there. Balancing on the guardrail and leaping six-foot of floor tiles to plunge into the deep end.

In summer I take a speedboat out in the bay. There's a big red one in the harbour that caters for tourists, churning up waves and spraying water in their faces. If I'm lucky with the reset, it's parked on the slipway with the keys in. Most times it isn't, but if it's not too far out, I untie a dingy and paddle out to it, usually with a six pack and some fish and chips swiped from one of a dozen outlets. I push the boat to its limit, bouncing over waves and turning tight angles, north, south and east as far as the confines of my world allows. And when I'm done, I either swim to shore or drive up on the sand – feeling like James Bond as I walk casually away.

The sun is my only friend now. People worshiped it in the past and now I understand why. I miss it when it's gone and glory in its return. It is the greatest pleasure of my new life – it's touch, like the hands of a warm-fingered masseur. And I can sunbathe for hours without consequences. Yeah I get burnt, but the next day it's like I've never been out. A favourite haunt for catching rays is the Spa's Sun Court when the orchestra's playing. All those blue and white striped deck chairs set out facing the stage, or the casserole dish as Josie calls it – on account of its shape. There's always programs lying around, but I rarely bother, instead grabbing one of their CDs from the admissions desk and playing it through the PA system. Sitting back then to enjoy the set with the sun on my face.

Occasionally, I do wonder what they're playing and look for clues. Some people are foot-tappers or head-nodders and by watching their shadows it's easy to get the tempo. With a little more difficulty, I can sometimes determine which instruments are being played by studying the orchestra's shadows. It's easiest with the violinist and drummer, due to the wide, often frantic movement of his arms and the projections of her bow. I say *he* and *she*, because I've been there for the glimpse, when the orchestra is revealed mid-tune. And their appearance comes with a wave of sound that echoes around the Sun Court for an unnatural period afterwards. As if my shadow world misses the orchestra as much as I do and has taken to weaving its own magic to prologue the notes.

One positive of this existence is that I find it much easier to live in the present – something Buddhists call mindfulness. I still spend a large part of my day thinking about my family, but in between I often drift into meditational states. Not having responsibilities can be truly liberating and some days I wander town like a child, becoming engrossed in whatever takes my fancy. I can spend hours reading in a book store, nosing around houses or walking the woods. And the more I engage, the less mental bandwidth I have left to worry with. If I'm feeling particularly low, I climb onto the rock armour that protects the harbour wall and make my way round the Marine Drive, jumping from rock to rock until I'm sweaty and exhausted. And whatever I'm worrying about evaporates – my brain's desire to keep me on sure footing, trumping any pointless brooding.

Now, when I said earlier that I was the only living thing in my world, that isn't entirely true. On occasion, I'm visited by a lone butterfly. The first one appeared while I was reading in the garden – fluttering into the corner of my eye as it made its way through Josie's well-kept flower beds. For a time, I was transfixed, and if I'm honest, overwhelmed – its sudden appearance, a sledgehammer of beauty in an otherwise sterile existence. I leapt up and ran inside, shouting for my family with the misguided belief I had re-joined humanity. My disappointment was immense. Since then, butterflies of all patterns and colours have visited me. Always one at a time and never more frequently. At first, I took to following them, hoping they would lead me to a portal back to reality. But if you've ever tried following a butterfly, you'll know it's a fool's game. A couple of minutes and you're apt to lose it over a fence or hedgerow. I don't know what their appearance means, but I've learnt to enjoy them – to stop whatever I'm doing and just watch until they depart – a period that can be as brief as a few seconds, or as long as an hour. In genetic terms humans and butterflies are miles apart, but I feel a profound bond with each one. Their multicoloured fluttering fills my heart in such a way that only someone in my predicament could understand. Lonely insect meets lonely human. Is it surprised and comforted by *my* presence, or doesn't it care? And why butterflies? Is it a clue to a way out, or another quirk of this limbo world?

For a time, I was obsessed with shadows, following them and studying them. Here's the sciency bit and if it's not your bag, you might want to skip ahead a few paragraphs...

For those of you still with me, the size and sharpness of a shadow depends on the size of the light source and the distance of the object from the surface it's projected onto. Hold your hand close to the ground and you get a sharp shadow. Move it further away and it becomes blurry. This is more obvious if you look at the shadow of something really tall, like a lamppost or tree. The blurry edges are in the penumbra which has a direct line to the light source and the strong shadow is in the umbra, which is blocked off completely. On a sunny day, shadows take on a blue tinge as they receive blue light unimpeded from the rest of the sky.

Whether you get a shadow on water depends on its condition. Clear water gives a clear reflection and the shadow is cast on the bottom. Muddy or rippling water gives no reflection but holds a shadow on the surface. One of those great examples of something you see every day, but don't process. Fascinating eh? Oh, and shadows are three dimensional – you can see this in fog when light breaks through clouds, the appearance of sun rays just an effect of the light being broken up by three dimensional shadows.

Dependant on the time, shadows are prone to exaggeration or underestimation, coming closest to the truth at mid-morning and mid-afternoon. Even then, they're distorted. With people it elongates their legs and fingers and shrinks heads. It's hard to tell someone's sex from a shadow and nigh on impossible to tell the breed of a dog or species of bird. Faint shadows, or those created by a high sun are difficult to analyse and some are just baffling. A surfer carrying his board is easy enough, but backpackers and mothers with babies often cast shadows that look like monsters. When interesting shadows presents themselves, I like to puzzle over them. Some are thoroughly inscrutable and there's often an ah-ha moment when the subject changes position, revealing its true identity. For example, I might see a shadow of someone leaning forward to the point of instability or someone doing press ups in mid-air – the objects supporting them shifted by the reset and its shadow now obliterated by the sun. Stranger, but more obvious are shadows cast by cyclists or passengers in open top cars that whizz by in various states of completeness.

Summer is my favourite time of year because shadows are stronger. Ironically, it's also the time when I feel most alone. Surrounded with hundreds of shadows is like being ignored at a party and I can feel myself ringing. As if my genes sense their demise and have resorted to broadcasting their existence. There's been several occasions when I've stopped to appreciate a view and the sun has broken out from behind a cloud, revealing a shadow alongside my own that's facing the same direction. In those moments I'm struck by a profound sense of connection and shared experience, so strong I believe it transcends my prison and touches the caster of that shadow in the same way.

Now the absolute weirdest things, I haven't mentioned yet. If I wake up in a location occupied by something at reset, I displace part, or all of it. Josie once moved our bedroom around, putting the bed against the chimney stack and a set of drawers in its place. I woke with my face squashed against woolly jumpers and extricated myself in a panic from what I discovered was the third draw down - scraping my face on a head sized hole. This, only to find myself suspended in thin air three foot above the carpet. I jumped up quickly and felt the air, but the invisible surface that had been supporting me was gone.

That leads nicely to the second thing – or to the *suspensions* as I've come to think of them. Inanimate objects, airborne at reset are frozen in place - hanging in the air as if suspended by invisible strings. And they stay there all day unless I touch them – whereupon they continue their previous trajectory. I once came across one of those demolition cranes with the big ball on the end. It must have been striking the wall at the reset time because all the bricks were frozen in mid-air. Another time I passed a church where a whole load of confetti was suspended in the air outside its arched doorway, unperturbed by the strong wind blowing through it. Some days there's hardly anything in the air and it usually depends on the weather and season. In summer there's footballs in the park and Frisbees at the beach and I've made a game of guessing which way they'll go when I touch them. Less desirable are the swirls of litter, joggers' spit and bird poo. I turned a corner last week and walked into a screen of the latter, getting it all over my cheek. In autumn, there's often great swirls of leaves suspended in the air – impossible works of art that glow red and gold when ignited by a low sun.

Rain and snow are my favourite suspensions. If it was raining at reset, the droplets are frozen in the air, as high up as you can see – producing hundreds of little rainbows when the sun comes out. And when the rain comes again, as it surely will, it strikes the suspended droplets sending water in random directions. When I go out in suspended rain, I take an umbrella. But instead of holding it above my head, I move it up and down in front of me, letting the drops run down the material and drip off the end.

When it snows, it's even better. Awesome in fact. The frozen snowfall is spectacular, but when it snows again, the fresh snow sticks to the suspended flakes, transforming them into snowballs that get bigger and bigger until they join up and collapse on one another. If it snows long and hard enough, the air becomes a mass of honeycombed snow you can't see through. On these occasions, I go out with my umbrella and use it in the same way, creating wondrous tunnels that Stevie and Maddie would love to play in. I once went out with the express purpose of getting lost – looping around and collapsing fragile snow tunnels until I was completely disorientated. It was fun at first, but I regretted it after a few hours, when I began to get cold and hungry. It was only when I brushed snow of a street name that I found my way back, feeling along forecourt walls and utilising my mental map of Scarborough.

So, to the big question: why am I here?

You might be thinking I'm dead, and this, some cruel lesson I have to endure before entry to the afterlife. A place in which I have no responsibilities, everything I want and no one to share it with. A world designed to cleanse me of materialism and align me with what's important. If so – it's working a treat. Those of you who subscribe to the ascendant belief that we're living in a super advanced video game, might be thinking I'm trapped in a glitch that shifted my timeline. If so, some higher intelligence could be working on the problem right now, preparing a software patch that will resync me with everyone else – returning me to my family, blissfully unaware of the last five years.

The truth is, I'm the victim of a shadow curse.

The week before I arrived here, I was browsing eBay for a Halloween mask. Halloween's a big thing in our house and I get a new costume every year, keeping it a surprise until the actual day. Scaring the crap out of the kids is something that never gets old. I can't remember the search term I was using, but an advert popped up for a Shadow Curse. *Buy it now* for a pound. Intrigued, I clicked the thumbnail and my screen was filled by an elongated shadow of someone set diagonally across the page. Thick legs thinning out to a smaller head. The text beneath read: Shadow Curse – eleven previous owners 657-2017. This was followed by a list of names, with Tom Martin at the top and Harold Arbrada at the bottom - presumably a name from the seventh century. I smiled. I love quirky things – especially those relating to the occult. So, interested to find out what, if anything would turn up, I bought it. I'd already committed to a 50-quid clown-executioner mask, so what was an extra quid?

I forgot all about it until Halloween came around and a manila envelope arrived on my doormat. I heard the clang of the letter box, but I was making coffee and didn't get to the door in time to see who posted it. There was no stamp and my name was hand written on the front in one of those old-fashioned calligraphy fonts. The envelope felt empty, but when I tore it open a shadow unfolded from inside, as if it had been held concertinaed by a powerful force. And like a sinister pop-up it leapt onto my wall, forming a larger version of the shadow that had graced my eBay page. The next thing I knew, I was waking up in Shadowland, furious at having slept in.

I'm sure then, this is the Shadow Curse and that I triggered it by opening that letter. Sounds ridiculous eh? But isn't this whole world I've been describing. Carl Sagan once said extraordinary claims require extraordinary evidence and if what I've experienced doesn't qualify, I don't know what would. But what should I do? Is my existence simply to be endured, or is there a way out? I worked on this problem for months - looking for patterns and clues. Was the 12.21 reset time important? A grid-reference? A flat number? A numerical representation of the letters L and K? If so, what did *that* mean? Or was it all about the glimpse? It's the one time our worlds line up, so perhaps there's a way of stepping through. For a time, I beguiled myself with the idea I was getting closer to a solution. But if truth be told, I got nowhere. I used to like puzzles, but I've thought about this one for so long I'm getting blisters inside my skull – a growing fraction of my mind, now a cemetery of bad ideas.

Everything changed though with the arrival of the Shadow King, approximately one year ago. I first saw him, or rather a likeness of him in Sainsbury's when I turned an aisle and was confronted by an enormous cardboard cut-out. The kind they use to promote upcoming films. This one was ten-foot tall and reminded me of a Darth Vader cut-out I'd encountered as a child. It depicted a stretched shadow with the words *The Shadow King - Coming Soon* at the bottom. Written in that same handwriting from the manila envelope. An advert for a Shadow King in a world of shadows couldn't be a coincidence and I knew this wasn't an advert for a film. It was a warning directed at me and it detonated in my bones.

Over the next few days, depictions of the Shadow King appeared all over town: as graffiti on walls, official posters in store windows and adverts on billboards. Some with the same legend as the first, others underwritten with *Beware the Shadow King*. The open-air theatre had an advert for him every day – one that transformed into a picture of a grinning boy band during the glimpse. Proof if I needed it that the adverts were solely for me.

A week later the caption changed to *Out 31st October*. A small change, but it felt like a countdown to some sort of reckoning had begun and it filled me with deeper dread. The date was a week away and it was all I could think of. When the day came there was a huge Shadow King painted on a bridge near my house, with the accompanying words: *Out Now!* I stayed under the bridge for some time, staring at the featureless, spray-painted face of the Shadow King, wondering what it all meant. The breeze was blowing litter across the park and the town beyond felt like an enormous hiding place.

I fought down a cowardly urge to run home and pushed on, telling myself that something new had to be a good thing. I crept through town, moving furtively from one shop doorway to the next, pressing myself against store windows to peer around corners. Eyes busy and heart racing - ready to sprint away at the slightest hitch.

It was hours later when I finally saw him – a timespan during which I'd relaxed a little and allowed my mind to drift. I had just climbed the steps through the Town Hall Gardens and had turned to take in the view across the South Bay. He was right there below me – walking the same stretch of sand I had just come from. A fifteen-foot, three-dimensional version of the images I had been seeing all over town, weaving through deckchairs and sandcastles. I ducked behind a wall, rising into a screen of foliage to watch him. He appeared to be tracking me – but my sandy footprints were mixed with hundreds of others and I couldn't understand how. But when he paused to pick up a Frisbee I'd knocked out of the air, and a few steps later, a ball I'd kicked at a sandcastle, I suddenly understood. He knew what the world looked like at reset and he could see the changes I had made. I've thought since how lucky I was to glean that information so soon after his arrival. As without it, I'm sure he would have found me that first day.

I watched him angle towards the road and step onto the path, hoping he'd lose my trail. But he didn't even slow. There was sand on my shoes and it had been coming off with every step, leaving a trail of fine grains he seemed to have no problem following. He stopped in the middle of Foreshore Road to look up, catching me off-guard. And despite the lack of detail in the dark oval of his face, his glare seemed to burn the foliage like a black searchlight. I ducked, tore off my sandy trainers and ran bare foot along St Nicholas Street, stopping at the corner with Westborough to look back. Panting for air with my heart thudding in my mouth.

The Shadow King appeared seconds later, as tall as the statue of Queen Victoria that stands alongside the Town Hall. But he came no further. He crouched to inspect my abandoned trainers, seared the streets with his black gaze and disappeared back down the steps. I waited for a few minutes before running back, bobbing down behind a queue of driverless cars. Wanting to be home, but needing to know what he was up to. He was back on the beach when I plucked up the courage to look down through the gardens again, heading towards the Lifeboat House. I skipped down some steps to get a better view and realised he was taking my backtrail. Could he find a way back to my house? I racked my brain, trying to remember all the changes I'd made to the reset. The cap I was wearing I'd taken from one of the beach vendors after spinning the rack and I'd reached around hygiene glass to dip a spoon in several flavours of ice cream a little further on. I ran down to the sea front and followed him at a distance, having to run to keep up with his big strides. He stopped at the hat stand and the ice cream vendor's, but when he reached East Sandgate hill, he just kept going. I'd come down the cobbled hill in clean trainers and he was now guessing which way I'd come. He was heading for the Marine Drive and I watched him disappear around the corner before jogging home.

The next day I hid like a coward. I'd been told to *Beware the Shadow King* and I was *bewaring* him like a six-year-old. In the end, I developed some testicular fortitude and went out – knowing I had to do something. I took my binoculars and made my way up to Oliver's Mount viewpoint – sprinting across open ground and hiding behind cars – the Shadow King's black gaze looking down at me from numerous billboards and graffitied walls. Once up there, he was easy to spot. He was walking along a terrace in the old town, his height enabling him to search two floors at a time. Solid to look at, but insubstantial and able to walk through walls. I went home and hid for the next week, scared what would happen if he found me. I ate what I found in the fridge, spending my days going from window to window and watching for him. I didn't dare go in the garden, watch a film or listen to music. And one night I awoke in a cold sweat from a nightmare in which he was standing over my bed, reaching for me with his long shadowy fingers.

But not knowing what he was up to soon became intolerable and I started going out, watching him from a distance and testing his capabilities. I tested his vision by releasing a bunch of helium balloons in Falsgrave Park then sprinting to the top floor bedroom of a nearby house with a clear view of the playground. I was barely in position when the Shadow King strode past the window, neck angled back as he watched them float away. He went right to the very spot on which I released the balloons, but I'd kept to tarmac and concrete and I was sure he couldn't track me. He turned a full rotation, his eyeless gaze passing over the window from which I peered. And then he left. Or at least I thought he had. I waited half an hour before moving and it was only by chance that I saw him when I glanced out of a lower window whilst making my way down the stairs. There's a steep bank at the rear of the park and he was standing inside a tree about half way up, with only his face and hands protruding. Waiting and watching. Ready to spring forth like a trapdoor spider. I left by the front door on the other side of the house and spent all day wondering what would have happened if I had gone out the back door and walked by that tree.

Another time I tested his hearing. There's a railway bridge down the valley we used to shout in on our way back from the beach, competing to make the loudest echoes. I let a firework off inside and the resulting bang brought him in under a minute. I followed him until sunset one day, needing to know if he continued his search for me at night. But as the sun dipped below the horizon he froze mid-stride, sinking into the tarmac as if it had liquified. I went to bed early that night and was back in time to see him rise with the sun, continuing his search as if nothing had happened. Three times now I've observed the same thing, sinking at sunset and rising at daybreak. And watching him on the beach one day, I noticed something obvious that I couldn't believe I'd missed. In a world of shadows, the entity that hunts me casts no shadow himself. Hmmm. I'm sure it's a clue and it's got my head hurting again.

Last week the Shadow King was lying in wait for me in Sainsbury's and it was only by sheer luck I saw him through the big front windows, his head sticking above an aisle, watching the front door. He must have found evidence of my previous visit and was hoping I'd return. I backed up on tiptoes, breath held like a mother retreating from a sleeping baby.

Throughout this period the *Out Now* posters of the Shadow King continued to appear. But a few weeks ago, the caption began changing again. *Join the cast before it's too late!* was the first change. A cryptic clue if ever I've heard one. A film's cast is the entirety of the people starring in it and in this context, the posters had to be referring to the cast of the glimpse. If so, its instruction is frustratingly redundant as that's what I've been trying to do since getting here! The *before it's too late* bit got me worried though, implying there was now a time limit to me joining the cast. And shortly after the adverts changed to *Hurry, while stocks last!* as if the Shadow King wasn't a single entity. Like every day was a new Shadow King and that his production line was running its last batch. The killer change was to *Last chance – Oct 31st.* As unnerving as his *Out Now* poster. I arrived here on Halloween and now it seems this entire insane experience is going to end on Halloween, five years on. But how do I join the cast? It's all I've been thinking about and I'm getting nightmares again.

I didn't know how to proceed until one day when I was standing with my back to the sun as it came out from behind a cloud. I watched as my shadow strengthened in front of me – *cast* by the brightening light. Another definition of cast is to cause (light or shadow) to appear on a surface. This world is filled with shadows cast by unseen people and yet the Shadow King doesn't cast one himself. The next day I followed him and I was there to see him disappear at the glimpse, as I had observed him do several times before. But this time I kept my eyes focused on where his shadow should be. At 12:21 it appeared as *he* disappeared – stretched out on a field between a bunch of kids playing football. *Join the cast before it's too late.* This was what it was the Shadow King's posters were referring to! His transient shadow was the cast I had to join. It was the portal I'd been looking for and my chance to re-join the world.

If I'm right, it's not going to be easy. I've got to creep up to the Shadow King and step into his fleeting shadow without him touching me. The *Beware the Shadow King* posters are still out there and if he gets his long fingers on me, I'm sure it'll be lights out or worse. My best chance is to run up behind him as he's walking into the sun. But I can't be sure he'll be travelling in that direction at glimpse time and I've only got a few days left. So, I've got a plan. I'm gonna set up a southward trail of items along the promenade from The Spa towards the old South Bay Pool. Then at noon, I'll blast some music from the bar to attract him. The idea is to follow him along a trail which will keep him facing the sun, running up behind him under the cover of music and into the shadow he generates at the glimpse. Simple. And no doubt completely flawed. But Halloween's tomorrow and it's all I've got.

If it works, there's no telling what the circumstance of my return will be. Will I be cast into the real world with years of absence to explain? Or will I return to my hall of five years ago with an envelope in my hands – the time I spent here wiped from my mind and my name added to that list on the curse's eBay page. In my mind's eye, I've imagined the former scenario a thousand times. The kids squealing their delight and jumping up at me. Josie frozen momentarily with her hand to her face, finally running down the path and throwing her arms around my neck - melting into our tearful huddle. But I know it's fantasy. I left them without a note and haven't made contact for nearly five years. I've missed birthdays, Christmases and parents' evenings and haven't sent a penny of support. I'm more likely to be met with puzzled awkwardness from the kids and simmering bitterness from Josie. And with no sane reason to explain my absence, there's a good chance I'd be estranged from my family the rest of my life. A man, people will say, who got fed up with his family and ran off to pursue his own selfish ends. Nothing could be further from the truth. So, I hope it's the latter scenario and I never have to face them that way.

I've often wondered what happened to the other people on that list, who were presumably trapped in a shadow world of their own century. Did they buy their curse from a market or a door-step seller? Order it from a magazine or newspaper? What did they make of the Shadow King and did any of them escape? Their shadow worlds must have been harsher than mine – especially that poor guy Harold Abrada from the seventh century. Living on your own's hard – but exponentially harder the further back you go. No double glazing and hot water for him. No supermarket rotisseries and ice cream dispensers. No mountain bikes and DVDs.

Now remember those butterflies I told you about. I went to the library to read up on them and discovered they were either extinct or unlisted. But I've got a feeling they were around for the others on the list and that they somehow crossed over from their world and their time. A nice oversight by whatever twisted intelligence or law of nature created our prisons – a weakness that has allowed symbols of hope to flow between us.

There's a good chance I won't return to this account, so you, the reader, may never know how my escape plan works out. I hope reading this you'll think more about what you buy online, and if you know someone who's missing, you might want to consider a shadow curse as the cause. And finally, to Josie, Maddie and Stevie – if by some quirk of fate you ever read this, know that I love you; that I was with you all those years and that I did everything I could to get back home.

Andrew Jons
In the shadow of Oct 30th 2010

Viewpoint

Tommo rode hard around the last bend, eyes fixed on the road and the trees blurring away to either side. He'd come up the steep end of the mount and he was hunched over his handlebars now and breathing hard; sweat running down his back. As he came in sight of the War Memorial he straightened to freewheel, veering onto the path which led to the viewpoint. At first it appeared he had the place to himself, but then he caught sight of a young man sitting beneath the monument, sipping from a gleaming hip flask. He gave him a polite nod as he leant his bike against the wall then stepped onto the right of two viewing platforms.

Bar a few wispy clouds the sky was unmarred and Scarborough was sweltering under a westering sun. The memorial stood a hundred and fifty meters above sea level and its elevation granted him an impressive panorama across town. From Throxenby on his left to the outer harbour and North Sea on his right. From South Cliff in the foreground, to the castle headland and beyond: a stretch of greenery that ran all the way to Ravenscar. For a time he was lost in thought as his eyes moved between familiar landmarks: the train station and the old windmill; The Sea Life Centre, lighthouse and Grand Hotel. The citizens of his shrunken hometown scurrying the streets like ants.

'Nice day,' said a voice beside him.

He turned to see the man from the monument step alongside him. He gave him a quick once over and decided he wasn't a threat. The *man* was actually a pasty late teen. Doc martins and drainpipes. Corduroy jacket over a t-shirt depicting a fantasy character. Metal hip flask now bulging in his top pocket.

'Everything looks so small doesn't it?' the man said, and there was a slight slur to his voice that suggested something stronger than coke in his hip flask. But his manner was pleasant enough. 'All you've got going on down there, shrunken to insignificance... Looks like you could reach out and touch it doesn't it? Like you could run your fingers along the rooftops.'

Tommo laughed. 'Yeah, I suppose it does.'

The man looked at him, considering something in the light of his semi-pickled mind. 'Can I show you something?'

'Depends what it is,' he replied, looking over his shoulder to the empty road and wondering what his intentions were.

The man read his concern and stepped back, showing his palms. 'It's nothing like that and I assure you, I mean no harm. I'm celebrating you see,' he said, tapping his hip flask. 'I've just finished a big project and I want to show it to someone.'

'Alright, but as long as I don't have to go anywhere. I only stopped for a breather and I'm about ready for off.'

The man smiled. 'You don't have to go anywhere, because where you're standing's right where you need to be.'

'Alright.'

'Look down at Scarborough again, but this time reach for it. As though it was a model instead of an actual town. Not too fast though – I don't want you to break anything.'

Fucks sake, thought Tommo. All he wanted was a few minutes peace and now this. The man was an obviously nutter, but he could see no easy way forward other than humouring him. So he decided to give him a few minutes, after which he'd make his excuses and leave.

He reached out and when his fingers struck a rough surface, he snatched them back in shock. 'The fuck's that?'

The man burst out laughing. 'Try again. You know where it is now. But go easy.'

Tommo reached out again, this time maintaining contact with the strange surface. He moved his fingers around and soon realised the sensation corresponded with the shape of the roof tops – as if the town had become a model of itself. He felt the turrets of The Grand Hotel and the castle walls, withdrawing as if he had caught himself exploring a corpse. 'I don't understand. Have you hypnotised me or something?' He looked at the young man with a new module operating in his head: a stranger-danger module that had started his heart racing. Innocuous nerd now a nefarious hypnotist.

The man blew a raspberry laugh and waved a hand, evidently finding his perplexity the height of entertainment. 'I promise you I don't know the first thing about hypnosis. If you don't believe me, you could always get on your bike and pedal away. You're free to go at any time. But you'll regret it later. As a rule I don't show my work to anyone. This being a one-time opportunity.'

Tommo had half a mind to do as he suggested, but his feet remained planted. 'Who are you?'

'I like to think of myself as The Model Maker, but my real name's Martin.'

'What did I just touch?'

'A dynamic model of Scarborough, built by yours truly.'

'But how?'

Martin raised his eyebrows. 'On one level I'd have to say I don't know. On another – that it's a bi-product of lots of hard work. You wouldn't believe the contortions I put my poor noodle through to make something like this. It's my second big project to date. My first being a similar model that takes it origin from the castle wall. A model of Scarborough viewed from the opposite direction and which includes Oliver's Mount.'

Tommo looked at him, torn between two choices. To bid this stranger goodbye or to reach for the model again.

He chose the latter.

'Here try this,' said Martin. 'Dip your finger in the sea – out there beyond the harbour. But do it slowly so you don't make a big wave.' Tommo followed his instructions and was surprised to feel the coldness of the water. He lowered his finger and it disappeared to the first knuckle before it struck something hard. 'That's the seabed and you won't be able to push through – no matter how hard you try.'

He brought his finger out, marvelling at its wet tip. But he brought it to his face a little too quickly, catching St Andrew church spire and snapping it off. The fragment landed by his feet, looking like nothing more than like a splinter of stone. He looked at Martin, expecting some form of chastisement, but the young man hadn't noticed. He was swigging from his hip flask and looking at the ripples his finger had made in the sea. Tommo took advantage of his distraction by bending to pocket the fragment.

'Why are you showing me this?'

'All that work and no one to share it with. I just wanted to see the look on someone's face. And besides, when you leave, I'll turn it off to public viewing. You'll never see me again and in a few weeks, you'll begin to doubt what you saw. Tell anyone about this without proof and they'll think your mad... So what do you think?'

'I don't know what to say. Impossible's probably the best word.' He took two steps to the left, trying to see behind the model. 'So where's the real Scarborough gone?'

'You're looking at it – try reaching for it again.'

This time his arm extended through thin air. 'I don't understand.'

'The model blends seamlessly with reality, replacing it at a single location: the very spot on which I created it and the very spot where you were just standing. Seeing you there, in just the right place felt like a sign and I was compelled to show it to you... Come back to where you were and you'll see the model again.'

He sidestepped and reached out again – fingers bumping against Valley Bridge. 'That's amazing!'

'Now look at the outer harbour wall. See anything unusual?'

'Yeah!' said Tommo, eyes narrowing to scrutinise the huge figure at the end: a huge statue of a four-armed behemoth, dwarfing the anglers beside it. 'What is that? I've never seen that before.'

'That's because it isn't really there. It's my trademark and it only exists on the model. It's a statue of Kring: a character from one of my favourite fantasy books.' He opened his jacket to reveal the character in full colour. 'If you move your head from side to side, you'll see him disappear and reappear. There on the model and absent in reality.'

'So it does,' said Tommo, performing several bird-like repetition. After a few cycles his eyes were drawn to the broken St Andrew's spire, which remained broken regardless of whether Martin's trademark character was there or not. He had no idea what this meant and he decided not to ask. This whole thing was becoming more surreal by the second and whatever rabbit hole he had fallen into, he wanted out of it. 'Look, I'd better get going before I stiffen up.'

'So soon?' said Martin, making no attempt to hide his disappointment.

'Yeah, but thanks for sharing,' he said, returning to his bike and swinging his leg over the saddle. With a goodbye nod he pushed off and left Martin gawping. Spokes blurring to invisibility as he rounded the bend.

Tommo took Filey Road into town, mounting the curb with amazement when he came in sight of St Andrews church. The top half of its stone spire was missing! The church door was open and there was a growing crowd looking up at the fractured stone. Some walking the perimeter in search of the missing piece and at times calling to others and shaking their heads. Seemingly baffled by the lack of wreckage. Tommo reached into his pocket to retrieve the fragment from the model and held it at arm's length. He rotated it to bring the broken base in line with church's broken spire and saw it was a perfect fit!

He had planned to go home, but now he biked down to the harbour instead. There was no fantasy statue guarding the entrance, but the anglers were still there.

'Did you see anything strange in the water,' he asked one after waiting for him to cast his line. 'About half an hour ago?'

'If you mean that big swell, then yeah. It seemed to come from nowhere. There was a big surge against the wall then nothing... D'you see it too?'

'Yeah, from over on the West Pier. But I thought you might have gotten a better look at what caused it.'

'Can't help you there,' the angler said, turning his attention back to the water.

When he got home, he looked at the broken spire under a magnifying glass and was amazed at the detail: the irregularity of the block faces, the moss, lichen and the bird dirt. The splintered wood and cobwebs on the inside. He had no doubt it was the church's missing spire and he sat there for almost an hour, mind stretching in several directions to accommodate what he was seeing. Interactions with the model resulted in real world consequences, and better yet, no one saw what caused them. No one at the church had seen a godly hand snapping the spire and the anglers hadn't seen a giant finger plunging the waves.

That night he was visited by a strange dream that flipped perspectives in the middle. At first he was moving tanks and soldiers around the childhood layout his mother made him one Christmas: a huge pegboard with pipe cleaner trees and paper mâché mountains; divided at its centre by a snaking river spanned by an underlay bridge with cable supports. He was firing matchsticks from heavy artillery when all of a sudden his perspective switched and he was reduced to one of the plastic soldiers he was firing on. As the matchsticks swept over his head a monstrous image of himself loomed over the mountains, reaching down as he ran for cover in a copse of pipe-cleaner trees...

The next day Tommo biked up Oliver's Mount again, hoping to see Martin and to get another glimpse of the model. There were several people milling around when he arrived and he waited for them to depart before stepping onto the right-hand viewing platform in the exact spot from which he had viewed the model. Martin had said he planned to turn the model off to public viewing, so he was surprised when his trademark statue appeared on the harbour wall and he was once more able to feel it. He watched for a time, but soon became bored – realising it was of no more entertainment value than looking down on the real thing. A dynamic model was meant to be interacted with. Otherwise, what was the point? He grinned, marvelling at the potential of what lay before him.

He took his keys out and removed a pair of fold-out scissors from the loop. Then with the blades closed he stuck the tips into a vacant patch of beach next to the lifeboat house and drew them across the sand. He had to weave through knots of holiday makers, but the tide was right out and he managed to avoid them. He lowered the scissors to survey his work and was pleased to see a long weaving trench with sand piled high on either side. Bristling with excitement, he mounted his bike and rode down the mount at a blistering pace. He went via the Esplanade and pulled up on Spa Bridge in awe. The trench was huge and its bottom filled with sea water. The expelled sand to either side was easily six-foot-high and there were people clambering up to look in. He rode down the snaking path of Olympia Gardens and onto the beach, dismounting where a woman was talking with three others and gesturing to the sand bank.

'What's going on?' he asked.

'This wall of sand,' she replied, her position on the beach leaving her ignorant of the trench on the other side. 'It rose all on its own, going from left to right in a couple of seconds.' She shook her head and stared at the monstrous wall that had obliterated her view of the sea. 'I've never seen anything like it in my life... I hope no one was hurt. There's kiddies all over the place.'

'Did you see what caused it?'

'No. It was like someone raked the beach with a big stick.'

More like invisible scissors he thought.

'I'm gonna see if anyone needs help,' she said, walking away with the other women in tow.

Tommo spent the next hour pushing his bike along the trench and looking in – watching police and council workers clearing people away and setting up cordons. Taking surveys and photos to who knew what ends. To know he was the author of such mayhem was immensely satisfying and he went about his observations with an insatiable interest. By the time the incoming tide reached the seaward sandbank, huge crowds had arrived to view the spectacle. For a time it looked like it would hold against the tide, until the waves swept up the area he hadn't reached with his scissors to attack the near side bank from the rear. Ten minutes later the seaward wall broke apart and the trench was soon swamped. And an hour later, all evidence of his mischief was lost beneath the rolling waves. But his delight was not to end there. The event was all over that night's news, local and national, with eyewitness reports and expert opinion. It was the best nights telly he'd seen in ages and he munched through a whole bucket of southern fried chicken with his eyes glued to the screen.

The next time he stepped onto the viewpoint platform, Martin appeared from nowhere. 'That beach thing was you, wasn't it?' he said, jogging up with a red face.

'I thought you were switching it off.'

'I tried – but it didn't work. You broke it when you snapped the spire off and I can't fix it. Why didn't you tell me what happened?'

'It was an accident.'

'Maybe. But that beach trench wasn't…. You're lucky no one was hurt.'

'I didn't know it would happen for real,' he lied.

'Well you do now, so stop. I didn't make this model for you to play god.'

'What *did* you make it for?'

He looked genuinely taken back. As if he'd never considered its purpose. 'Because it's what I do. I like to watch. It's more interactive than you've seen. I can rotate it with my mind and zoom in and out. I don't interfere though.'

'I see. So you're a creepy voyeur?'

Martin frowned. 'I wouldn't say that.'

'Like a kid watching a train set then. What a waste.'

'Look. I don't have to justify myself to you. I want you leave right now and never touch my model again!'

'Alright, alright, I'm going,' he said, mounting his bike under Martin's hot gaze. 'It's all yours.' Then he rode away, turning at the bend to see Martin glowering after him.

But he wasn't to be deterred that easily. Especially by a spoilt weirdo who was barely out of nappies. He was back on the viewing platform the next day at dawn, armed with binoculars and tweezers. If Martin was trying to fix the model's on/off switch he was determined to have some fun with it first.

He watched the cars crossing Valley bridge and when they stopped for the traffic lights he reached out with his tweezers, plucked a little red Peugeot from the road and put it down inside the castle walls. He switched to his binoculars and brought the car into focus – hands trembling with excitement. At first there was no movement in the car.

He could see the driver, but she was completely frozen. It only occurred to him now how jarring the short trip must have been and he began to think he may have caused a whiplash or even a broken neck. He estimated the direct line from bridge to castle to be around a kilometre and he had transported her there in about two seconds. A lightening acceleration from a dead stop. When the door opened and a wobbly-kneed woman staggered out, he breathed a sigh of relief. She was looking around as if she had arrived in Wonderland and Tommo broke into a fit of laughter, wondering what on earth she was thinking. He watched her make her bewildered way to the barbican and disappear into the gatehouse shop – presumably to make her vehicular trespassing known to the staff. He watched until a police car arrived, feeling a little bit guilty when they took her away. He went online again that night and the top story on local news was: Castle Visitors Startled By Falling Car. The article featured testimonies from a group who were strolling the headland when a car dropped from the sky and a dazed woman stumbled out. Rumours were circulating on social media that it was part of an elaborate publicity stunt and the driver was being questioned by police as to how she gained access to the grounds.

Tommo was up the mount again early the next morning with a rucksack of sundry items and a head full of ideas. So far, he had interacted with and taken from the model. Today he would try adding to it. He had a list of ideas ranging from replacing the castle with a model of Sauron's tower, to part submerging a model dinosaur in the South Bay. The potential was mind boggling and he was all but pissing his pants in anticipation.

He reached into his bag, deciding to start with his Jelly-Baby idea. He opened the packet and extracted a powdery pink one. Then, trying to keep a steady hand, he reached down to the beach. He found a section big enough to accommodate the base and screwed it in with a delicate motion. He let go tentatively, fearing it might fall and to his relief it remained in place – the thumb-sized Jelly Baby now a hundred-foot monstrosity towering over the sands. He lifted his binoculars and trained them on the scene with sniggering excitement. What he saw through the lenses was way beyond his expectations and it was like watching something from a Stephen Spielberg film. His focus fell first on a group of terrified beachgoers whose necks were angled back and who looked ready to run. He blurred right and stopped on the money shot: an arc of people staring up at a pink mass so big, he could only see its base. For to look at the Jelly Baby's head through the binoculars was to get a background of the West Pier and lighthouse. He wondered if they recognised the Jelly Baby for what it was. Up close and at that scale he imagined they were more likely thinking alien invasion – those now fleeing the beach no doubt fearing the opening of a hissing door in its powdery pot belly. He thought it would be funny to block the exits from the South Bay with Lego bricks and was reaching into his bag when he was startled by a whiny shriek. 'Hey – I told you to stop!'

He looked up to see Martin storming down the path, face flushed crimson and hands in fists. He gasped when he saw the monstrous Jelly Baby on the model and made to snatch it away, checking his anger in the last moment to lift it carefully and toss it into the ferns below the platform. 'What's wrong with you? This isn't a toy and you're not God!'

'Oh, come on,' Tommo said. 'It's just a bit of harmless fun. You should have seen it. It's has to be the funniest thing I've ever seen.'

'It's not funny! It's really not. What you're doing is irresponsible and dangerous.'

'I was careful.'

'How do you know there wasn't a little kid down there? Half buried in the sand or squatting in a hole.'

'There wasn't.'

'You sure? You aren't, are you? What you're doing has attracted attention. I got a visit last night from people who know what I do. They suspect me in these shenanigans and they want me to stop. I didn't tell them about you, cos there's no telling what they'd do if they found out I gave a stranger access to my model...God what was I thinking? I must've lost my mind.'

'Nice try kid. Likely story.'

'You don't understand. If you don't stop, they'll kill me.'

'Nice knowing you then.'

His reply seemed to strike Martin like a slap because he lunged forward, shoving Tommo in the chest. 'Bastard!'

Tommo shoved back harder, sending him sprawling. But he shot straight up and charged with wind milling arms. Tommo weathered the blows and hit back in a cooler and more targeted way, landing a punch square on his nose that almost sent him tumbling over the viewpoint wall.

Martin sagged, nursing a bloody nose with streaming eyes. 'That's your last chance!' he said and stalked away. 'Someone's got to stop you.'

'Good luck with that.'

Martin spun, blood patting onto the dirt track. 'Remember, this isn't my only model!'

'Whatever. Go play with that one then.'

Tommo watched Martin disappear around the corner with his hand held to his face, switching between jogging and walking. He turned his mind back to the model and considered his next move. He thought about replacing the Jelly Baby but decided it wouldn't have the same shock factor. He saw a little spider on the wall and on impulse swept it up. He reached out to drop it in St Martin's Square, stopping himself just in time when the consequences of such insanity suddenly dawned on him. The spider was tiny, but it would be a huge Shellob-like horror to the people of Scarborough, who it would no doubt see as prey. Putting the frighteners on his fellow Scarborians was one thing, but he didn't want to kill anyone. Besides, he had to go down there himself and he wasn't fond of spiders.

When he spotted the children in Gladstone Road playground, he took a tube of Sherbet from his bag. As a kid he used to tip his head back when it rained, sticking his tongue out to catch the drops and wishing it would rain sugar. It never happened for him – but it was going to happen for these lucky kids. Whilst looking through his binoculars, he reached out with his free hand, tapping the tube with his finger and causing Sherbet to rain. The children stopped playing to look up, and to his delight some had closed their eyes and were sticking their tongues out. He saw he'd given some too big a dose as they were waist deep in the stuff. But that only inspired him to tap the tube harder, sending heavy cascades down on the whole playground and covering most children to their necks and several dinner ladies to their waists. He knew he'd gone too far when some began crying in their struggle to pull free. And only then did he consider how much time it would take to clear up and what a gloopy mess a heavy rain might make of it. He shook the last of the Sherbet down his throat and tossed the empty tube into the bushes.

He rummaged in his bag, pulled out a little Thomas the Tank Engine model and placed it in the train station, next to a platform of waiting passengers. It was three times bigger than the train they were expecting and from what he'd read about the car he placed on the castle headland, it would seem as if it had appeared out of thin air. The resultant shock it caused was piss funny, more so as he pushed it out of the station - its moon face fixed and grinning and its immobile wheels scraped through the gravel on either side of a track it didn't fit. What tickled him most was the contrast in reactions. The adults were backing up and pulling their children away, overwhelmed and terrified by the blatant wrongness of the huge plastic train. But the kids were loving it – pulling their parents back and twisting their necks from retreating pushchairs. It was Thomas the Tank Engine from the telly and his impossible appearance and improbable size served only to amplify their awe. This was better than anything they'd seen at a theme park and they wanted to touch Thomas's shiny blue sides, to hear him whistle and blow smoke from his chimney. The children up front were looking at its face as if expecting him to speak and Tommo wished more than anything that he could make that happen. If the train's giant moon face uttered even a single word, he could see their parents fainting as they squealed with delight.

It was only when he got bored and lowered his binoculars that he saw the flashing light from the castle wall. Something catching the sunlight on and off – as if someone were signalling him with mirror glass. He raised his binoculars again and ran his magnified view over the castle until he reached the viewing platform. There beneath the castle's English Heritage flag was Martin and he was looking straight at him – fist upturned with a vertical middle finger.

Remember, this isn't my only model.

Only now did Tommo understand the significance of Martin's parting words and why he spoke them like a threat. He had another model of Scarborough which took an opposite viewpoint and which included Oliver's Mount. A model he had no doubt Martin could interact with. Tommo lowered the binoculars, flushing cold at his vulnerability. As he stared over, something rose from the viewing platform, resolving into a reaching hand that soon covered Scarborough in a vast shadow. In a matter of seconds he was looking up at the cracks and whirls of Martin's godly fingertips. He turned to run, but he was standing on a dynamic model with no place *to* run. No place he couldn't be reached by that hovering hand. He took three strides before Martin's index finger plunged, squashing him against the memorial steps like a bug - his pulverised body turning instantly to sludge.

The police were phoned an hour later by an elderly couple who found an open backpack close to a stinking mess which appeared to contain human teeth. For the next week the memorial was sealed off while a forensic team went to work. DNA analysis eventually linked the sludge to a missing man, but the manner of his death was only ever guessed at. Had they flown over the mess the investigators might have seen an enormous fingerprint. A fingerprint that could be scaled down to match a harmless young man who lived with his grandma in the old town and whose bedroom was overflowing with maps, models and comic books.

The grim remains were reported in the local paper, but the report was overshadowed by a slew of fantastical stories including: a rain of Sherbet at Gladstone Road School, the fleeting appearance of an enormous pink figure on South Bay sands and an oversized Thomas the Tank Engine at the train station. The lead article was a compilation of all strange occurrences of the last week with speculation they were the work of a visiting magician. There were calls for the prankster, once revealed, to be jailed. And given their evident and considerable means, it was generally agreed they should be forced to compensate the town.

When the memorial was reopened a young man with a corduroy jacket and Doc Martins was the first to visit. He took a tiny church spire from his pocket and reached out, attaching it to its rightful place. Then he waved his hand, breathing a sigh of relief at the resultant click.

Sand Script

Joe stopped and stared at the writing in the sand. He was halfway through his morning paddle, ankle deep in foaming water with the sun shining over his shoulder. The words were about a foot tall and they faced out to sea: *Help me* - presumably scrawled by someone using a stick or fingertip. He smiled and was about to turn away when he remembered the tide was going out; which meant the damp sand on which the writing was scrawled had been underwater a few minutes ago. He looked up and down the beach for the author. He was directly opposite Spa Bridge at the centre of a vast arc of sand. It was a little after 6.30 a.m. and there were only a few people out: an old couple practicing their golf swings, a jogger in a visor and sunglasses, and two dog walkers. Any one of them could have left the message, but he had been walking towards this spot for the last ten minutes and should have seen them. Then again, his mind was apt to wander when he was paddling, his gaze usually fixed in the marbled water three foot in front of him. So, with a mental shrug, he left the improbable letters behind and soon forgot about them.

That night he dreamt. He was standing in the same spot on the beach, but there was no Spa Bridge and no roundabout beneath it. Instead there was only the Valley, thickly wooded with a narrow track leading out. The sand was studded with boulders, the largest just beyond the reach of an incoming tide. An iron loop was fixed into its seaward face with a set of manacles running through it. Alongside the boulder was a rickety boardwalk. One end buried in the sand and the other extending into the water on seaweed strangled supports.

129

His attention was snatched by a group of people emerging from the track. Perhaps fifty by the time they were gathered on the sand. The groups apparel was of a different age – most of the women in russet gowns and white wimples; men in linen shirts and tunics. One woman stood out. She was dressed in a spotless white gown and her hands were bound behind her back. A pair of beefy guardians bookended her - vice-like grips encircling her delicate arms as they manhandled her across the sand. The group was led by a bearded man, dressed in a severe leather jerkin and red doublet; pleated hose, stockings and brass buckled shoes. Chain of office around his neck. He unrolled a parchment as the Woman in White was forced to her knees before him. Her guardians' rough hands biting into her narrow shoulders.

'You have confessed to riding a winged beast across the South Bay, naked and smeared with blood... You admit to possessing a malignant touch which you administered to three boys: you stroked the head of Tom Wildrow; shook the shoulder of Billy Bartle and pinched the ear of John Milton. All three took ill under mysterious circumstances soon after and were dead in under a week... You foretold the collapse of the Castle wall, the Osowan shipwreck and the sickness that decimated Falsgrave... Foretellings heard by dozens of witnesses...

'In your wretched hovel was found the potions with which you poisoned Falsgrave's water supply... Etched into your walls were discovered the spells with which you brought down the castle wall, drew the Osowan onto the rocks and summoned the winged beast... Most damming of all, examination of your person revealed the mark of the devil on your right shoulder and a withered teat in your nether regions... A teat bearing evidence of recent suckling.' At this last there was a collective gasp from some of the witnesses and one woman swooned and had to be steadied. 'You have been found guilty of witchcraft and sentenced to death on the Drowning Stone... Do you have anything to say?'

There was a break in the clouds as he asked his question and the woman's white gown appeared to glow in the strengthening light. She raised her face as if to answer but turned to Joe instead. And though her face was pale and her eyes raw from crying, it did nothing to corrupt her beauty. She was perhaps the most beautiful woman he had ever seen. 'Help me!' she implored. 'They hurt me and made me confess. Those potions are naught but medicines and the writing on my walls, Greek. Taught me by my Da.'

The official seemed not to hear or even to have noticed she'd turned her head. He lifted his damming gaze now and spoke to her handlers. 'Fix her to the Drowning Stone.'

They dragged her to the boulder on her knees, gown bunching up and ploughing the sand. The sea was lapping at the boulder now and she gasped as they forced her to sit in the flow while they untied her hands and set them into the manacles. When they stepped away, she tried to stand but the chain arrested her movement with a metallic scrunch and she splashed back down with another gasp.

The official jumped up on the rock to look down at her as she struggled. 'The chain won't allow you to stand, but it has freedom enough for prayer. Place your hands together while you still can and pray to the Lord. Perhaps *He* will save you.' And with that he jumped down and joined the others who were filing on the rickety pier in order to witness her demise.

The tide came on inexorably - wave after wave soaking the Woman in White ever higher. She strained against the manacles with wide eyes, lifting at intervals into an awkward crouch she soon had to maintain. An agonising effort that was clear in her face. The sea swelled until it covered her shoulders, the muscles of her neck roping and her collar bones jutting as she strained to stay above the flow. The first wave to slap her face had her coughing and spluttering, then screaming for help. But she soon had no spare air with which to vocalise, her last breaths snatched in the troughs between waves, her eyes tight shut as the peaks washed over her face. Before she disappeared for good, she opened them one last time to look directly at Joe, the terrified whites relaying her plea better than anything she could have said: *Help me!*

Now *Joe's* eyes snapped open and he jerked forward in bed, arms reaching for her. But it was just a dream and it faded like a spent firework, leaving him to the darkness of his room: his wardrobe and drawers, his pile of dirty washing and his weight bench. All draped in midnight shadow. It took him some time to settle and when he finally got off, he entered a dreamless sleep that served him till morning.

The next day, he went paddling again before work. He began from the Spa and as he kicked through the waves, he kept his eyes glued to the spot where he'd seen the writing. The tide was further out, but the writing was there again. Just shy of the dying waves, on a patch of sand that was only just beginning to dry. He looked around, not just along the beach, but along the road and up at the myriad windows of the Grand Hotel, sure someone was having a laugh. That he had been singled out for some elaborate practice joke and that there was someone filming him from afar. But it was only a few seconds before he dropped the idea. No one could have predicted what time he would come paddling by and the writing had to have been done in the last few minutes. In the time he had been watching. He bent to cup some sea water in his hand and poured it on the letters, obliterating three quarters of the H and the top of the E. Proving to himself that it wasn't some sort of magic water-proof writing before stomping it out completely. He finished his paddle, jogged home and went to work. But his attention was like a broken searchlight swinging in the wind and he spent most of his time staring through his computer screen and thinking about the Woman in White.

That night he was back in the dream. But this time, the complicated neurology that directed it decided to go with a horror edit. The scene was the same, but the sky was boiling with grey clouds which raced across the sky. The precession of locals arrived in slow motion – faces like chiselled wood except for the frightened, elfin face of the prisoner in white. She turned to him with pleading eyes so raw they almost ran with blood, silently mouthing *Help me*. When they forced her to her knees, he got a close-up of her bound hands and saw the horrifying damage wrought by their thumbscrews: her cracked and splintered nailbeds, swollen to bloody pulps. His dream cam took the Woman in White's view as her litany of crimes were read and he found himself looking up at the bearded man as the grey clouds boiled behind his head. There was no mercy in his severe countenance and as he spoke, red fire bloomed in his avid eyes.

When she was dragged to the Drowning Stone, he realised he had taken her place completely. He felt *his* knees grooving the sand and their rough hands digging into *his* arms. He gasped as they forced him to sit at the foot of the Drowning Stone and the icy North Sea soaked through her dress. Felt the bite of the manacles as they were clamped onto his wriggling wrists. He was left struggling against the cold metal as the hard-faced witnesses filed onto the boardwalk - some breaking into smirks as the first waves slapped his face. From his sea-level perspective the six-inch waves were an onslaught of tsunamis and he strained to stay above them – matching his panicky breaths with their peaks and troughs. In time even the troughs were too high and he was forced to remain crouched in the frigid flow – mouth tight shut and head tipped back. Drawing desperately through his nose. When the first wave inundated his nasal passages, he inhaled straight into burning lungs...

Joe woke choking and gasping, confusing the darkness of his room for the murky shallows of the North Sea. He sat up and clicked on his light, cursing the writing on the beach for getting into his psyche.

Unlike the previous night, he didn't sleep easy afterwards and the next morning he forfeited his morning paddle for an extra hour in bed. When he finally rose for work, he decided to avoid the South Bay until he got the sandy letters out of his head.

He slipped out of the office on his lunch hour to fetch a sandwich and on impulse paid a visit to the Maritime Heritage Museum. There were two volunteers on duty: one tapping away on a computer in the back and another out front - fixing up a display of old Scarborough pubs.

'Hi. I wonder if you could help me. It's probably a long shot, but do you know if there was ever any witch executions on the South Bay? It'd be way back in the 16th century or thereabouts?'

'Never heard of anything on South Bay, but that doesn't mean there wasn't. From what I've read, hangings and the like were done at Gallows Close - where Sainsbury's now stands. Before that, who knows. Why do you ask?'

'Just following up on something someone said. Dinner party stuff that got me curious. What about witches in general? Were there any famous cases in Scarborough?'

The man smiled. 'It's not something I'm ever asked about. We mostly deal with maritime history. You could try the library.'

Joe had forty minutes of his dinner hour left, so he took his advice. A helpful librarian directed him to a Local History section and he had a rummage around. But all he found was a brief mention of an alleged witch named Anne Hannan who was eventually acquitted. No mention of any witch executions on the South Bay or anywhere else.

That night and every night for the next week, Joe suffered through different versions of the same dream – each with its own unique horror. One night he was beneath the waves, looking into the Woman in White's face as she inhaled seawater. Another time he was left looking into the faces of the witnesses as they watched her drown – their sadistic smirks and laughing eyes, soundtracked by her gasps and splutters. The only consistency between versions was that at some point the Woman in White would look at him; pleading for help. And by the end of the week Joe's eyes were as red as hers and he couldn't concentrate at work.

'Who are you?' he asked the shadows of his room when he woke for the seventh consecutive night.

The next morning, Joe decided to go paddling again, needing to see virgin sand along the tideline. It was over a week since he last saw the writing and he thought its absence would go a long way towards putting his mind to rest. If it wasn't there, he could put it down to an elaborate trick. But it *was* there and as he came upon it, he spun away with his hands to his face - like a man who has happened upon the body of a dead relative. He turned back to the writing with a wash of fear and racing heart, needing to confirm what he had seen. There in fresh letters above the retreating waves was the name *Alwyn*. He was still holding his face and now he almost unhinged at his knees. It was the answer to last night's question and proof he was going mad. In a spurt of anger, he stomped the writing out with his bare foot, face contorting as if it were burning him. But as he stepped back into the sea to survey his work, an invisible finger began to scrawl familiar letters into the newly compacted sand – until *Help me* was once more staring up at him. It was such a challenge to his sanity he uttered a noise he didn't recognise. A watery yelp that came from somewhere deep in his chest. His whole body was trembling and was starting to feel lightheaded. He turned to walk away but thought better of it when he saw a woman and her dog coming towards him along the shoreline.

'Morning,' he said when she drew close, raising his hand and trying to convey a calmness he most certainly didn't feel.

'Morning,' she replied, angling up the beach to go around him.

'Have you seen this?' he asked in a wavy, school-boy pitch. The hand he pointed with was shaking and he was starting to feel giddy.

She drew up at a distance, looked at the sand then back at him. Eyes speculative and cautious. 'What's it say?' she asked. The writing was upside down to her and he realised she couldn't read it. But at least she could see it. Proof it wasn't all in his head.

'Help me.'

'Oh,' she said, looking for her dog as if fearing for her safety. It was early, the sea-front shops were closed and the nearest people were way down the beach.

'I just thought it was weird,' he said, trying to sound casual and unthreatening. 'Writing like that, so close to the sea as it's going out.'

'I guess so,' she said. 'Most likely kids... Well, I best be going. Have a nice day.'

'Yeah, you too,' he replied, realising how he must sound.

She walked away and he went the opposite way. He sat on the Lifeboat House wall to put his trainers on and jogged back home.

He rang in sick to work and to his surprise his boss laughed. 'About time,' he said. 'You've looked terrible all week.' He advised him to take a few days off. To book a doctor's appointment and to get a good night's sleep. This last recommendation *Joe* almost laughed at. Going to sleep was the last thing he wanted, because he knew Alwyn was waiting for him on the other side.

He did take his boss's advice to book a GP appointment though – but he had ten days to wait so he decided to do some research. He discovered the causes of nightmares included: eating too late, antidepressants, blood pressure medication, narcotics and sleep apnoea. None of which applied to him. Nightmares could also be caused by a stressful event which could be treated with counselling. Presumably to dig down on the cause. But how could he tell someone about the writing? They'd think he was crazy. The only way to convince them would be to show them and he couldn't imagine a councillor in the whole of England that would take a paddle with him at 6.30 in the morning. He gave up on the internet and paced his front room all afternoon, trying to think of what a councillor would say if he somehow convinced them he wasn't mad. It all came down to the letters in the sand and their recurring *Help me* plea. But how could he help someone who, if she ever existed, had been executed hundreds of years ago?

He went to bed that night with great reluctance. He'd read nothing about the effect of alcohol on nightmares, so he had a large red wine as a night cap. It seemed the dream was waiting for him behind his eyelids, so soon was he on that beach again. The dream went through a familiar form up until the moment Alwyn was hauled to the boulder and manacled in place. This time she didn't struggle as the tide came in. Instead, she simply held her arms up so the chain dangled, mouthing the words *Help me* until the water covered her face. He did not awake from this nightmare, but he remembered it in the morning and knew what he needed to do.

After breakfast he went to the hardware shop on Victoria Road and bought a hacksaw. It was the most expensive one in the shop and it had a red plastic grip. He took it down to the beach, feeling a strange mix of certainty and incredulity about what he intended and wondering what the hell he would say if a policeman searched him and asked what he intended to do with it. He was much later than usual, but he set about his paddle, hoping he would find some writing. He wasn't disappointed. It wasn't yet school holidays, but the beach was sprinkled with picnicking families and young children who were racing up and down the sands, brandishing spades and swinging buckets. Rushing in and out of the sea and jumping waves. The tide was all the way out and there was no one close to where he found the writing – as usual just shy of the water line and directly in front of Spa Bridge. This time there was just a large letter X, as if Alwyn knew his intention. He stopped, pretending to look inland as the water lapped at his ankles. But really checking to see if anyone was watching. There were several people on the Grand Hotel's balcony, some of whom were looking down. Likely many more looking out of the hotel's windows. But that was always going to be the case. He slipped the hacksaw out of his pocket, keeping it hidden behind his forearm as he crouched by the X. He dug a hole in the centre about ten inches deep, laid the hacksaw in and covered it over. Then he stood and looked around self-consciously. *There*, he said to himself, feeling instantly better.

He went to bed tired and uneasy, the events of the day clinging to his mind like ivy. But to his surprise, he drifted off in minutes and slept through to his alarm undisturbed. The best night sleep he'd had in ages. Deep and rejuvenating kip that had him whistling over his egg-on-toast breakfast. And so it went on for the next few weeks and his experience on South Bay became distant and foggy – a bizarre experience he began to write off as a mix of hallucination and misremembering.

It was a whole three months later when he walked into the Maritime Heritage Museum, where the same volunteer he'd spoken to last time was fixing up a display titled: The Witch of South Bay.

'Hello,' said the man as he finished Blu-tacking the poster.

'I see you dug out some witch history.'

The man looked puzzled. 'This one's hardly off the wall... People can't get enough of her.'

'Really? Who is she?'

'You're kidding right?'

'No. I've never heard of her.'

'You can't be from round here then. Alwyn Meadows was her name and she's all visitors want to know about. They want to see her Drowning Stone and they're always disappointed when I tell them it's gone.'

The name struck Joe like a spear and the mention of a Drowning Stone turned him white.

'You alright?'

'Yeah, sorry. I don't feel well all of a sudden.'

'You wanna to sit down or something?'

'No. I'll be alright,' he said through a narrowed throat. 'Go on. What else can you tell me?'

'Well, I expect you've heard about the old witch trials. When all those innocent women were put to death on the grounds of spurious evidence and forced confessions.' Joe was glazing over, but he nodded him on. 'Women whose only crime was to be old or isolated. Scapegoats blamed for everything from a bad harvest to an outbreak of warts. Well, the same can't be said of this un. By all accounts Alwyn was the real thing. Not that I believe in all that supernatural stuff. But she was a real nasty bugger. The story goes, she lured two brothers to her shack with promises of sweetbread; rendering them unconscious with one of her potions instead.' The man was warming to his theme and his eyes were beginning to sparkle.

'They woke trussed up in a wooden cage full of old bones. In the name of some bizarre ritual, she cut the toes off one boy and cast them into her fire. Then she took the other one out to drown him. Lucky for him, his brother escaped and hobbled on bloody feet to get help. They found Alwyn under a full moon at the far end of the South Bay, dunking the poor lad in a rock pool. Just in time to save him. Alwyn was charged by a local court and sentenced to death on the Drowning Stone – which we believe was washed away or removed some time in the 18th century.'

'I'm sorry, I'm going to have to go,' said Joe, feeling a sudden surge of nausea.

'Oh, alright. But I was just getting to the best bit.'

'Do you have any information I can take away?'

'Certainly,' he said, reaching for a Perspex holder and pulling out a pamphlet. 'This'll tell you all you need to know.'

He took the pamphlet and whirled away, rushing outside to throw up in the gutter.

Back home Joe opened a bottle of red wine and emptied a full glass in three gulps before taking the pamphlet from his pocket and studying the drawing on the front cover. It was a historic drawing with little detail, but the figure portrayed as the witch bore no resemblance to the woman from his dreams. He opened it and read the inside cover, trying not to look at the drawing on the second page. He skipped through the parts the man in the museum had told him about and slowed up to read the last paragraph:

Alwyn Meadows was tried for witchcraft in 1654 and sentenced to death by drowning. She was manacled to the Drowning Stone on the South Bay sands and left to the North Sea. Witnesses to her execution watched until she disappeared under the rising water. But when the tide turned and the Drowning Stone re-emerged, Alwyn Meadows was gone - the chain that bound her cut clean. Dozens of children went missing in the years after and Alwyn Meadows was often blamed. Many claim to have seen her walking the rock pools when the tide is out and the full moon is riding high.

Joe's hands were shaking by the time he looked at the picture on the opposite page. The wooden mouth of the valley, the huddle of witnesses and the bearded man with his chain of office were straight out of his dream. Alwyn Meadows was front and centre, chained to her Drowning Stone and waist deep in seawater. The boardwalk was there and there was even a mark on the sand where they had dragged her to the stone. It was a simple drawing, but the artist had captured his dream perfectly. Perfect except for the witch herself. The woman depicted was the same one from the front cover: the typical old crone of witch lore and not the beautiful Woman in White from his dreams. He scrunched the pamphlet in a fist and threw it in the bin, his mind a vortex of guilt and incomprehension: *What had he done?* competing with *How had he done it?* The simple explanation was that he had finally lost it and was living through an altered reality of his own making. But the pamphlet was tangible evidence it was more than that. Last week Scarborough had no famous witch and now it did. That he had changed reality by burying a hacksaw was a heinous hypothesis which if true was worse than going mad. He brought the remaining wine to the front room, finished it off and started on another, trying to create a sane narrative in his increasingly intoxicated mind. In the end the alcohol got the better of him and he sat down to stare, his thoughts nothing more than the shifting of charred wood in a dying fire.

When he finally went to bed, he was so drunk he faceplanted on the duvet and was asleep in seconds. His dream was waiting for him as if he had collapsed through a trapdoor. This time Alwyn was nowhere to be seen in the line of people that filed out of the woodland. She had been replaced by a withered husk of a woman who was attired in a filthy grey dress. Her black hair hung well past her shoulders, threaded with tiny bone fragments and knotted with grass twine. As she was manhandled across the beach she looked at Joe with licentious fire, sticking her tongue out as if to lick him. As she passed the man that would read her sentence she drew harshly through her nostrils and spat a nasty globule into his face, causing him to stagger away in revulsion, wiping at the offending gloop with his fancy sleeve. Retribution was swift and she was stuck hard across the side of her head by one of her handlers and forced to her knees. As her litany of crimes were read she regarded the official with bare faced hate, voicing an unintelligible sermon which forced the bearded man to raise his voice ever higher.

Alwyn was dragged to the Drowning Stone and when the manacles were secured, she began to laugh - a shrill, hysterical sound that spiralled around her like autumn leaves. And when the tide reached her bony breast, she dipped her head to the foaming water and sucked some up – ejecting it in a big spout that she aimed at the witnesses. Throwing her head back and generating a leonine roar that had no right coming from her slender frame. 'I've seen your faces and I'll be back for your litters. Mark my words and be warned.' After this she began to chant in her unintelligible language, clanking her manacles until she was submerged. The witnesses made their way off the boardwalk and filed into the trees, the only evidence of the Drowning Stone, the cresting white water that ran over it. The last person disappeared into the woods and the branches settled behind them.

Joe's view began to change, drifting downwards until he was looking over the surface of the sea. And for a time he hovered there, waves rolling through him and dying on the shore – their frothing death throes and gurgling backwash punctuated by the screech of distant gulls. He was descending into a profound calmness when Alwyn resurfaced with a gasp, almost nose to nose with him. Her wet hair covering most of her face and her one visible eye blazing triumphantly...

He jerked up in bed to be confronted by a ten-foot version of Alwyn's face, superimposed on his bedroom. She had been waiting for him and she began to laugh in that leonine register – a disdainful rumble that shook the room. His suitcase fell from his wardrobe and several pictures crashed to the floor. He scrambled back up his bed, mashing himself against his headboard in an attempt to put distance between them, hands held up defensively and eyes prolapsing their sockets. At this Alwyn lunged forward, green tongue slipping from her cracked mouth to give him a long spectral lick. He swatted her way with a yelp of terrified disgust and was fighting empty shadows well after she disappeared.

In time he sat over the side of his bed, his mind intoxicated with a disorienting mix of alcohol and dream residue. He righted his night lamp then sat with his head in his hands. He began to cry and then sob – his frustration and helplessness leaking out of him in a series of shuddering waves. When it reduced to a low whimper, he laid back exhausted, head contacting something hard in his pillow. He twisted around, reached into the slip and pulled the offending article free -

throwing it away with a cry of horror the moment he clapped eyes on it.

There against the skirting board, shining in the glow of his nightlight was the hacksaw with the red handle. It was rusted with age, but he knew beyond doubt that it was the very same one he had buried on the beach. And as if to confirm its authenticity, Alwyn's laughter started up again: spiralling around his head until he began to scream.

A Rubbish Bank Holiday

August bank holiday and Scarborough's South Bay is packed. Three thousand visitors burning a million calories per hour under a blistering sun. The traffic on Foreshore Road stops and starts, stops and starts, progressing no quicker than the bustling hordes of pedestrians. Queues grow outside beach kiosks, lured by the aroma of fried meat and onions, or the images of ice creams on display boards. Above and all around, gulls shift on their perches, eyeing the crowds and making ready to swoop for the next spilled morsel.

Children ride coin-operated machines outside arcades: a red boat, an aeroplane, a laughing giraffe and a flying saucer. A little girl mounts a pirate ship with a 99 cone, bawling at her father when the ride surges to life and a blob of ice cream, along with its chocolate flake, tumble down her pretty pink top. Nearby, a man with a full arm tattoo whacks an electronic punch bag into its housing and is rewarded with a satisfying ding. He turns a grin on his leather-clad girlfriend who coos in appreciation.

Flashing lights and candy delights
Beach nibbles and ice cream dribbles

On the beach, hundreds of families have laid claim to patches of sand with windbreaks and towels – the web of space between them negotiated by newcomers seeking their own place in the sun and those questing for snacks or toilets. The less thoughtful kicking sand at sunbathers who lift their heads to glare. Distant vistas shimmer in the heat and shade has become a precious commodity; rising in value with every passing hour and causing some to look enviously at their neighbour's beach tent and parasol. Sunbathers rotate like sausages as their unprotected skin is ravaged by a remorseless sun. Some are becoming human lobsters, caught every which way by their varied antics. Those who've fallen asleep have caught only on one side and those in t-shirts and hats have developed crimson collars and sleeves. Fifty square meters of sunburnt skin and rising.

Bodies flex and wobble in varying degrees and bare feet race over hot sand, seeking the relief of towels or abandoned footwear. Voices combine and cancel so only squeals of delight stand out in the background drone. Beachballs arc between patting hands and fuzzy softballs travel between Velcro mitts. A chiselled youth, who looks fresh from ancient Sparta, strikes a moody pose for a group of giggling girls. Close by, a large gentleman, who looks fresh from ancient Rome, rests against an enormous beach bag, munching grapes.

On a stretch of vacant sand, a frustrated boy runs with a length of twine, trailing a languid dragon kite he insisted on buying, despite his mother's warning that there was no wind. He sprints past a little girl who is returning wet from the sea, her bright face morphing into a scowl when she discovers her scrawled heart defaced in the most appalling way. Her initials are untouched, but those of the boy she likes from piano lessons have been replaced by those of a nasty one who lives up her street. She turns a full circle, sees her grinning brother and charges him with a spade.

On the shoreline, children dig channels from the sea back to their sandcastle moats - standing behind the battlements like kings and queens until they're swamped by the tide. Abandoning the slumped ruins, they return to parents who dry them off - the brush of towel like sandpaper on their legs.

All heads turn when a gang of overheated teenagers charge down the beach and champagne dive, surfacing with cold-shock gasps and raucous laughter. Beyond them, people float on lilos and rubber rings close to a flock of idle seagulls who bob insouciantly on the undulating waves. Further out, a speedboat of delighted passengers churns up white water as it steers around the pirate ship Hispaniola. Scarborough is at its picture-postcard best, shimmering in an air of care-free fun and lazy recreation.

Posers and dozers
Sunstroke and warm Coke

Sun-drunk and weary visitors head back to hotels and fresh ones flock to replace them. Those departing take tiny quantities of sand with them: trapped between wet toes and hair, in the folds of damp towels and screwed-up swimwear; in the bottoms of trainers and the grooves of flip flops. Sand which will later be shook out in back yards, vacuumed from car seats and swilled down plug holes of distant towns. But it's not what the visitors take away that damages the beach - it's what they leave behind. For the most part those vacating the sands leave only footprints, water-logged holes and slumped sandcastles that will soon be erased by the incoming tide. But some have left more permanent evidence of their visit, despite the numerous Keep Your Beach Tidy notices and open-mouthed bins they passed to get here.

Across a half-mile crescent of seething sand a shame of litter is building: Styrofoam chip trays and soiled serviettes; broken buckets and snapped spades; paper flags and alcohol wipes, sun cream bottles and drinks cans; bag loads of lolly sticks, chip forks and cigarette butts. In the shallows beneath the waves are two pairs of broken goggles and several pairs of broken sunglasses. Floating on the surface: a set of punctured armbands and several filthy plasters.

But the day isn't over and the rubbish accumulates at a steady rate.

On the Lifeboat House wall, two teenage girls flop down with Cornettoes in hand. They tear the wrappers off in careful spirals before looking around for a bin. The nearest is fifty yards away on West Pier. It's a short walk, but too far in this heat. One of them shrugs and lets the paper drop to the sand in front of a boy who is digging a hole. He looks at the fluttering spiral and frowns at them. But the litterbug just giggles and turns to her friend who soon follows suit.

On the promenade an Elvis lookalike flicks his cigarette butt onto the sand before putting his face to the coin-operated binoculars. A couple in hemp shirts and bucket hats finish their fish and chips and without compunction, bury their vinegary trays and chip forks in the sand. A girl in a flowered swimsuit runs to her parents to whine about a punctured lilo currently drifting beyond the waves. Her father sits up in irritation, a hairy arm held to his forehead to shield his eyes. 'Leave it,' he says in a voice that brooks no argument. 'We'll get another one tomorrow. Just play in the waves for now.'

In front of Olympia Leisure a mother reaches for her pram after changing her infant's nappy, cursing when she realises she's forgotten the nappy bags. She eyes the hole her six-year-old just got bored of and, after looking around for disapprovers, drops the loaded nappy in and covers it over. Beneath the Spa, a group of teenagers play three-a-side rounders, lubricated by several beers. A young man is caught out and drops down by his girlfriend who consoles him with a hug and an expression of faux sympathy. He slugs the last of his cider and belches, throwing the empty can over his head with no intention of retrieving it.

In the middle of the beach, a family of hungry day trippers have succumbed to the relentless aroma of fish and chips. The mother is already in pursuit of their ten-year-old twins and the father has been left to pack up. He's got the beach gear crammed into his backpack and there's only the tent to pack away. He searches the crowd for his wife, looks back at the tent and decides to leave it. He's hot and irritable and it looks like a ball-ache to pack away. His conscience is quieted when he imagines some kid putting it to good use, and if not, the council clearing it away. It's what they're paid for isn't it?

Trippers and tippers
Spending cash and leaving trash

At five past one, a series of fault lines appear in the sand. A whole swathe of beach from the Lifeboat House to Olympia Leisure suddenly sags several inches, causing walkers to misstep. Almost everyone feels it and even those prostrated in the sun raise their heads. Some stand for a better look – eyes following pointing fingers to the ominous cracks. There's a spectrum of reaction, ranging from nervous laughter and shrugged shoulders, to stony-faced concern. Some turn to strangers for answers:

'Did you feel that? / What's going on? / Has this happened before?'
'Sure did / No idea / Not in my lifetime.'
'What did you think it was?'
'Slippage / Settling of layers / Buggered if I know.'
'Do you think we're safe?'
'Dunno/ Best ask a lifeguard/ It'll be right.'

But the sand is solid now and the event seemingly over. The kids have already forgotten about it and they are back to digging holes and building castles. Most adults soon follow, lathering on sun cream and turning their attention back to celebrity magazines and crosswords. Sinking back into pleasant daydreams and idle chat.

Ray-Bans and sun tans
Paperbacks and sandy cracks

At ten past one, there's a commotion at the water's edge: bathers rushing from the sea and pointing to deep water. An area beyond the breakers is boiling and foaming as if a giant shower head were being held to the surface. Soon almost everyone is on their feet, entranced by the strange spectacle. As they watch the sand shifts and sags again, but this time it doesn't stop. It's most evident higher up the beach as one by one the stone blocks of the promenade wall seem to rise from the sand, as if something is being pulled out from under the beach. People stagger and fall; others drop to all fours. A collective gasp is followed by calls for distant children and several nervous screams.

As the beach stabilises, huge geysers of sand erupt from various places as tentacle-like arms break the surface and thrust skyward. As the sand disperses the stunned and bug-eyed beachgoers study the arms in the full light of the sun. They're stretched to the height of lamp posts and appear to be comprised of rotten fish scales chorded with twists of multicoloured plastic that run their whole length like veins. Bottle caps and ring pulls stud their surface like shiny warts. The arms relax now and snake the air; their plastic components scrunching and creaking. The idyllic afternoon has morphed into a nightmare and the crowds are suddenly unified in terror. Most race for the promenade, others to the water's edge to gather children. The arms whip down coiling around fleeing limbs and dragging their owners to the dark holes that spawned them - yanking them beneath the sand with an awful snapping and crunching of bones. Recovery teams will later conduct an extensive and costly search, but they will never be found.

Snaking arms replace seaside charms
And petrification's the new recreation

The father who abandoned his beach tent loses sight of his family in the panic and drops his bag to join the exodus, jumping sandcastles and weaving through parasols – into the crush of people surging for the promenade. The Elvis lookalike is slower to react and he grips the railings with white knuckles, staring into a hole down which a little boy has disappeared. It's only when an arm reaches for him that he breaks free of his trance. But it's too late. It reaches between the top and middle rail, circling his waist and yanking him forward. He strikes the railing with a thud and cries out, his back arching obscenely as his waist is pulled through the gap. Something cracks in his spine – the strength goes out of his legs and his bladder and bowel let go – soiling his jeans as blood oozes from his mouth. Another yank and the arm cuts through him in a spray of blood, the two halves of him collapsing in a bloody pile.

The chaotic exodus is in full flow when something huge rises from the frothing sea, generating a three-meter tsunami that sweeps up the beach with such speed that no one on the sand escapes. It's like being struck by a syringe-press of water and they are propelled forward in an aquatic melee of bodies, deck chairs, prams and parasols. The wave reaches the promenade wall and passes right over; waist deep to the fleeing pedestrians. It goes out in all directions, crashing against the West Pier and the twin harbour walls simultaneously. It deflects upwards in great fans of white water the likes of which Scarborough's worst winters have never seen, thundering down on fleeing families and washing them into the harbour.

Those with the luxury of an extra few seconds begin to flee, clambering onto cars and up lamp posts. Stranded drivers brace for impact and can do nothing but wind their windows up – the music from their radios obscene in the face of the oncoming wave. The crowds, packed tight now, race across the road, the lucky ones escaping up staired alleyways to higher ground in Eastborough: up Lifeboat Steps and Rowing Club Steps; up Gilly's Steps and New steps. Some with babies and toddlers gripped to their chest. Others with no responsibility but to themselves, taking two or three steps at a time. Most run into shops, cafés and arcades, for no other reason than there's nowhere else to go. The wave courses over Foreshore Road with its baggage of beach detritus, lifting cars and motorcycles, tables, chairs, Zoltan machines, penny pushers and cuddly-toy grabbers.

Those finding an exit to second floors are lucky. Most aren't. The wave boils viciously over deep-fat fryers before striking the back walls of those ground floor businesses with a watery wallop that drowns all in its grasp.

The wave hits the Futurist theatre as though it were a sea wall, sloshing up Blands Cliff to the first turn of its cobbled road and catching dozens of fleeing holidaymakers. The backwash pulling most from their feet and drawing them into its frothing retreat. Those beyond reach watch in stunned silence - some with hands to their mouth and others with camera phones out. Diners in first floor restaurants press tight to windows as their fish and chips and posh lattes go cold. People line Spa Bridge, cluster on the Grand Hotel balcony and crowd Olympia Gardens; gawping at the monstrosity that generated the wave. At first it is hard to discern any detail due to the sandy seawater cascading from its angles. But by the time the wave reaches the arcades its form is revealed for all to see. A litter leviathan has risen from the sparkling waters of the South Bay – a mutant monstrosity whose head is a grotesque hybrid of fish and crab. Its disc-like shoulders are draped in fish nets and studded with glinting metal which later video analysis reveals to be ring pulls, coins and wire.

A tourist army flees the tsunami
Last breaths and watery deaths

The monster utters a guttural sound that rattles windows and scatters gulls – a note that communicates anguish to all that hear. The spent wave retreats in a great streaky froth that moves cars the other way, the occupiers gripping their wheels in terror. People are swept back to the sea, those upright and conscious able to appreciate the leviathan as they are drawn inexorably towards it. The monster raises three new appendages from the slosh, each terminating in what looks like a crab's claw, but fashioned from flattened beer tins. They extend outwards beneath its huge fisheyes. The one on the left goes for a knot of visitors packed into the lower station of the Central Cliff Lift. Its metallic cutter opens ten-foot wide and closes in a blink, severing three people at the waist. Then it moves further in, sounding like giant scissors as heads roll and blood sprays. The central claw snips at those on the Rowing Club balcony who are unable to retreat due to the weight of people behind them. The one on the right goes for those on the West Pier, snaking around cars to reach its victims. The claws move left and right, forwards and backwards over the retreating water - snipping heads that rise above the froth and smashing through high windows to slaughter diners who had thought themselves safe. Cars are cut open like tins, the occupants shredded in a flurry of blades. One man, emerging soaking wet from an arcade, sees a clawed arm reaching for him and runs inside to hide behind a cuddly-toy grabber. The blades open and close cutting through machine and man as one. Some who escaped up alleyways creep back with the retreating water to help or gawp, realising their mistake only when a set of blades (turned at an angle to fit into the passage) reaches in and cuts them in two. The monster's blood-shot eyes observe the carnage from way up high, its quivering mouth spewing a decade's worth of cigarette ash.

Snip snip snip go the beer-can blades
Now who cares about buckets and spades?

When the targets dwindle the claws withdraw beneath the waves, to be replaced by several seemingly limitless tentacles that exude a rank odour of rotten fish, soiled nappies and vinegary scraps. But these tentacles are not fluid like those of a squid or octopus. These are powered by chords of metal and plastic held together with a glue of fish scales and they pucker and crinkle as they snake over the bay, squealing and popping as they buckle and hinge. The longest reaches for Spa Bridge sending people running for the Esplanade. But this arm isn't seeking fresh prey. It reaches over the bridge and loops back under – spiralling around itself to form a firm grip. A second arm snakes into the roundabout beneath the bridge and loops over the wall to take a similar grip. A third shoots up to the Grand Hotel, smashing through a bedroom window and into a high corridor, doubling back through another room and smashing through another window to take a hold on itself; sending shards of glass tumbling onto residents fleeing the balcony. Meanwhile, a fourth arm takes hold of the lifeboat house and a fifth reaches up through the town hall gardens to take hold of the Queen Victoria statue. A sixth coils around the Lighthouse like a living helter-skelter. Three more reach up alleyways, smashing through shop and café windows on Eastborough and anchoring themselves on the terrace. Nine arms in all, holding the South Bay in a death grip.

The monster issues a cry of white-hot fury and begins to pull. The arms tighten like bowstrings and the sound of tortured plastic and metal blend with screams of terrified tourists. The rails on Spa Bridge begin to buckle, supporting walls fail in the Grand Hotel and cracks appear on the lighthouse. Shop fronts collapse on Eastborough and the Queen Victoria statue starts to lean. The monster pulls harder still, its netted body lifting several feet out of the water. Its eyes bulge as it surveys its creators with one final baleful glare before exploding – raining tonnes of rubbish across the sea front.

Several competing sirens can be heard as emergency vehicles arrive on scene from either end of Foreshore Road. But they are too late for most people. They were informed en route of a major incident on the sea front – their switchboard swamped with babbling and terrified callers with fantastical reports of a giant sea monster. Thought initially to be pranks but too numerous to ignore – the screaming in the background adding weight to their claims. The responders are too late to see the litter leviathan and most will be too busy over the coming hours to see the video footage that is already circulating the globe. They exit their vehicles to look upon a perplexing and horrific scene.

There's water running out of shops and arcades and draining from cars parked at strange angles on the road, despite a calm sea whose modest waves are breaking gently on the sands. The whole sea front is festooned with rubbish and covered with a fine ash. Plastic bags hang off gutters and car roofs and windscreens are covered with cigarette buts and chip forks. The air stinks of fermented trash and rotten fish. But this is only background for the true horror. Bodies and body parts are strewn everywhere, dozens of corpses floating face down in the sea and many more sprawled in the retreating waters amongst thousands of drinks cans and Styrofoam cups. Cries for help spur them to action and a policeman vomits when he sees a severed torso wrapped around the railings. A paramedic runs to the nearest body and finding her deceased runs to the next. People are exiting their vehicles and stepping over bodies. Other are sloshing through the water in a daze, some without mind to the rubbish hanging off their shoulders. Film crews arrive within the hour to document the event, but much of their footage is deemed too graphic to appear on mainstream TV.

It will be over a week before the sea front is cleared of bodies and waste. Scientists are at a loss to explain what happened, but the internet is replete with theories. Some say it was an alien invasion; others that it was an elaborate hoax. But those who were here to look into the monster's eyes know better. Among the survivors are the couple who buried their chip trays, the father who abandoned his beach tent and the teenage girls who dropped their Cornetto wrappers. They were close enough to read the brand names on the monster's plastic veins, to hear the snip of its metallic crab claws and smell the stink of its explosion. They heard its mournful cry and were left with no doubt that it was born of the many years of littering to which they had participated. And it would be a long time until any set foot on the sand again.

It was a rubbish bank holiday
But the South Bay had its say
The dead were mourned
And the litterbugs transformed

Scarecrow's New Friend

They were on their way out of the charity shop when Ollie's mummy stopped to look at a blue jacket with big black buttons on.

'Why don't you go look for a book while mummy looks through this rail?' she said. 'Last one, I promise.'

Ollie walked the bookshelves, slowing up when the assorted sizes and bright colours signalled his arrival at the children's section. The books were loosely packed and he browsed with fascinated eyes and sticky fingers, pulling out those with exciting covers. He settled on one with a dog in a cowboy hat and sat cross-legged to look inside. But just as he was making himself comfortable, he caught sight of a more interesting book that was positioned face out on the shelf. There was a man with a sack face on the cover and he was attached to a post with his arms out to the sides. Straw fingers sticking out of his torn shirt. The sun was out and the sack-faced man looked happy – his ragged mouth fixed in a broad smile. But it wasn't the cover that drew Ollie's attention, it was the bits of cardboard projecting from its edges.

He slid the cowboy-dog book off his lap and took this other one down. It was big, but much lighter than he expected. He opened it at a random page and was surprised when a figure of the sack-faced man rose from the page. He had seen a pop-up at school, but hadn't had the chance to operate it. He caught up now – opening and closing the page quickly and slowly, peering at the folding mechanism and wondering how the little man didn't get crumpled up.

He was opening another page when his mummy gripped his shoulder. 'What you got there Ollie?'

'A pop up.'

'Let's see,' she said, taking it away and opening random pages, so far above his head he couldn't see. 'What a lovely book. And only a pound. Shall we get it?'

Ollie clapped his hands and they took it to the elderly lady who was pricing clothes at the front counter.

'Just this,' his mother said.

'Ah, the scarecrow book,' the lady replied. 'It came in only yesterday. I remember because it appeared at the back door all on its own. Most people donate whole boxes or bags of stuff. A beautiful book though. Such lovely colours and so well preserved, despite all the names written inside. We get a lot of kiddies books, but far too many with scribbles and torn pages. Pop-up books are usually the worse, but this one's immaculate. And it looks hand made. Notice there's no price or barcode.'

'A bargain for a pound then,' his mummy said, picking through her purse and dropping a coin in the lady's hand.

They went food shopping afterwards and Ollie forgot about his new book until his mummy brought it to his room for story time. He was sitting against his Avengers pillow with his nightlight glowing through its Pooh Bear shade. She sat on his bed and produced the forgotten book from thin air, her mouth open in a *look what I've got* way.

'Scarecrow's New Friend,' she read from the cover.

'What's a scarecrow?'

'It's a big doll stuffed with straw that farmers use to stop the birdies eating their crops. They think it's a real person and it scares them away.' She pointed to a row of birds on the cover. 'These are crows and that's why it's called a scarecrow. Because it scares them away.'

'What's crops?'

'All the lovely vegetables the farmer grows.'

'Like potatoes and carrots?'

'That's right, and all the green ones you won't eat,' she said rubbing his tummy. 'Like broccoli, cabbage and peas.'

'EEEERRRR!'

She opened the book and a cardboard mechanism unfolded to produce a bent-backed farmer sowing seed into furrows. Nearby several crows were perched on a pop-up fence, watching with interest.

The farmer is out sowing seed,
But the crows are hungry and need to feed.

'Pull the tab Ollie,' she said, pointing to a piece of cardboard projecting from one side. He did as asked and the farmer's arm lifted, producing a row of seeds in the furrow. She pointed to a little flap on the soil which he opened to reveal a wiggly worm.

The next page was a pop-up of the crows swooping down to feed on little green shoots. Ollie pulled another tab and the shoots were all nibbled and full of holes. He opened a big flap to reveal the farmer in the distance, running towards the birds and shaking his fist. 'Oooh look,' his mummy said. 'Mr Farmer's really angry.'

'Cos the birdies are eating his crops?'

'That's right... I wonder what he'll do.'

She turned the page and an enormous scarecrow rose from the centrefold. The farmer was off to one side with his sleeves rolled up, admiring his work with his hands on his hips. And the crows were back on the fence looking glum.

The farmer wants his crops to grow,
So he's made a great big scarecrow.
To stand there all night and day,
keeping those pesky crows away.

The next page was a mid-summer scene with the scarecrow pop-up at the centre again and pull tabs and window flaps all the way around. When Ollie pulled the top tabs the farmer's crops rose from the ground: sweetcorn, potatoes, broccoli and carrots. When he pulled the side tabs, bees and butterflies wove through the crops and little mice ran across the field. He opened windows revealing the roots of a corn plant, a winking spider and a juicy slug. The farmer was out with his watering can and by rotating a cardboard disc, Ollie made sprinkles of water appear. The scarecrow hung proud over the scene and when he pulled another tab it swayed, causing a row of nervous looking crows to crane their necks.

'Such a beautiful book,' his mummy said before lifting it to her nose. 'And it smells nice too... An outside smell – as if you were actually there.'

She turned the page, activating a pop-up cart heavily laden with vegetables. The farmer was bent over, about to cut the last pumpkin from its vine. Ollie pulled a tab, swiping the farmer's knife and cutting it free.

The crops have grown,
From the seeds that were sown.
The farmer's chuckling,
Cos his old wagon is buckling.

Scarecrow rose from the next page, but this time he was alone in the field without even a crow to keep him company. There were no crops in the fields, except for the ragged leaves the farmer had left behind. It looked cold in the field and Scarecrow was looking across to a pop-up farmhouse full of warm light – his smile replaced with a downwards slant. You could see through the farmhouse window to where the farmer and his family were making merry around a dining table laden with food. Their faces aglow with the light of a blazing hearth.

Scarecrow worked hard on the farm,
Keeping the crops safe from harm.
But instead of taking him home,
They'd left him all alone.

'Aaaww look,' his mummy said. 'They're having a party and haven't invited him. They're all warm and he's out in the cold. This farmer's a bit of a meanie, isn't he?'

She turned the page and a close-up of the scarecrow's face jumped out. She gasped and Ollie's eyebrows jumped half-way up his head. The scarecrow's burlap face was sucked in around his mouth and his black eyes were narrowed to slits. It was like a scary mask Ollie had seen an older boy wearing for trick or treat last Halloween.

'Oh my!' his mother said. 'I wasn't expecting that. Scarecrow doesn't look happy. That's pretty scary don't you think?'

Ollie nodded his agreement, sucking his fingers in wide-eyed fascination.

When Scarecrow popped up on the next page, he was walking across the field to the farmhouse. Back hunched and straw fingers curled into claws.

As winter grew cold,
Scarecrow grew bold.
They'd left him out to shiver,
Now they'd cry him a river.

The next page was flat and showed the scarecrow outside an open bedroom window, with a little boy sleeping inside. Ollie pulled the slider and a flap turned on the page. The bed was suddenly empty and the little boy over the scarecrow's shoulder. When his mummy didn't turn the page, he looked up to find her staring at the flap. 'I think that's enough for tonight,' she said, closing it. 'I thought it'd be fun, but it's getting scary and I don't want you having nightmares. I'll have a look at it later and if it's not too scary, we'll finish it tomorrow.'

'Awwww.'

'Come on, lie down.' She tickled his tummy and tucked him in, finishing with a kiss on his forehead. Then she left with his new book under her arm, pulling his door until it was almost closed. Ollie turned onto his side and fell asleep sucking his fingers and wondering what happened to the little boy.

His mum took the book through to her bedroom and flopped on the bed to finish it. There was only one more page and it showed Scarecrow taking the little boy to the field and mounting him on a crucifix of lashed branches. There was a cardboard tab which made a search party appear and at the same time transformed the boy's head to a burlap sack and his hands to straw. The search party was comprised of farmer and his family and they were looking for their boy, but seeing two scarecrows.

> **They're looking for Little Tim,**
> **But they'll *never ever* find him.**
> **Scarecrow made another new friend,**
> **So it turned out well in the end.**

The tone of the final page was of a happy ending. The scarecrow was smiling, but the little boy wasn't. His hollow eyes were vacant and his rip-of-a-mouth, ragged and downcast.

She puffed and frowned, unable to take her eyes from the pop-up scarecrow whose evident ecstasy was captured in his repose: his straw fingers extended and his head tipped back; taking the sun on his smiling sack face. *That's how it ends!* she though: *In revenge for being left out in the fields, Scarecrow kidnaps the farmer's son and turns him to straw.* She stared at this last page, trying to process the books sudden decent into darkness and wondering why the author would go there.

She flicked back to the front, looking for an age recommendation. But the first page had no information besides a list of hand-written names beneath a single line of text: This Book Belonged To. *Belonged* instead of belongs. This struck her as strange and it made her think of the book's penultimate line: **Scarecrow made another new friend.** *Another* new friend, despite him making only one.

She concluded that the book had no publication information because no sane publisher would release it. Not these days anyway. She had read some gruesome fairy tales as a kid, but modern tastes had changed. She had to admit it was well made though. It's beautiful pop-up mechanisms opened with the crisp freshness of spring flowers and the hand-painted illustrations were so vibrant they almost shone. Whoever made it had talent, but they had a lot to learn about child psychology. She tossed the book onto the floor, but one last look at the cover made her reach for it again. There was no author name. Just the title and a picture of the happy scarecrow. She looked through the book once more but couldn't find the author's name anywhere inside. And when she turned back to the cover the scarecrow seemed to be mocking her.

When Ollie returned from school the next day, he asked his mummy if she'd read him the rest of the scarecrow book. But she told him it had been a mistake to buy it. That it was a big boy book and too scary. Hearing this made Ollie mad, especially since she often praised him for being a big boy. He followed her around the kitchen while she made tea, trying to unsuccessfully to change her mind. And he protested to such a degree over the dinner table that he was sent to his room without desert. When it was time for his bedtime story, she chose one of his favourites, about a frog who finds a water pistol in his pond. When she sat to read, he told her it was for babies and that he wanted the scarecrow book instead. But his mummy wouldn't budge and he ended up going to sleep without a story.

The next day Ollie decided to read the scarecrow book himself and set about trying to find it. He checked the shelves downstairs, looking for its distinctive spine to no avail. When his mummy was busy making tea, he sneaked up to her bedroom and found it lying by her bed. He took it to his room and flicked to where they broke off two nights earlier – the page with the flip flap that showed Scarecrow taking the little boy from his bedroom and putting him over his shoulder.

Ollie turned the page to see two scarecrows and pulled the slider to see the boy transformed – his head to a sack and his hands to straw. He wondered what it was like to be turned to straw and if the boy still had a face underneath the sack. He read the last few lines – lips moving as he sounded out the words. Then he looked at the faces of the search party; especially the woman who he thought must be the boy's mummy. She looked sad and frightened because her face was streaked with tears. The scarecrow just wanted a friend, but he had done a bad thing taking the boy. Because how would he get back with his mummy if he was made of straw? He read the penultimate line again, unsettled not by the word his mother had been focused on, but by the word in front of it. **Scarecrow *made* another new friend**. Ollie would often tell his mummy that he'd made a new friend at school, but it was never in the way Scarecrow had made his new friend. Scarecrow actually *made* a new friend by turning the boy to straw. He looked at Scarecrow's face and saw he was happy again – like in the first pages when he was looking after the farmer's crops. Little Tim wasn't though. His black eyes and sagging mouth looked really sad – as if he was missing his mummy and didn't want to be made of straw. There wasn't anymore pages and Ollie wondered if Little Tim would be able to call for her with his sack-cloth mouth. Looking at the picture made him feel a little bit funny in his chest and tummy. Like being poorly without being sick. He was still staring at the picture when his mummy entered the room to fetch him for tea, her smile vanishing when she saw what he was holding.

'I can't believe you took that from my room! That's naughty. Well I hope your happy now. If it gives you nightmares, it's your own fault... Don't ever go into my room like that and take things without asking.'

It was fish fingers and beans for tea and they ate opposite each other without talking. He looked over twice when reaching for his water and she simply shook her head. He swung his legs beneath the table and made sure he ate everything on his plate.

He played with his figures in the evening, the scarecrow book forgotten and abandoned on his desk. When his mummy helped him to get washed and ready for bed, she was in a better mood and he could tell he was no longer in trouble. They went to his room and she took down another one of his favourite books – about a pirate who couldn't remember where he'd buried his treasure. He laughed all the way through partly because she did all the faces and the actions. But mostly because she was no longer mad at him.

As he was drifting off, he turned to his desk and was surprised to see the pop-up book laid open with Scarecrow upright on the page. He wondered how it had opened and thought his mummy must have done it when she put the pirate book away. It was dark in that corner of the room and although he couldn't see the detail of the pop-up scarecrow, it felt like he was looking at him. He turned away and closed his eyes, but there was a fuzzy feeling on the back of his neck that wouldn't go away. He sat up and thought about calling his mummy to shut the book. But he knew it might make her mad again. So he got out of bed and went to his desk on tip toes, flipping it shut and scampering back. Diving beneath the blankets like a flat fish burrowing in sand.

When he finally got to sleep it wasn't the forgetful pirate that visited his dreaming mind. It was the scarecrow book. In the dream the book was huge and he was standing on the pages amongst the giant pop ups as the slider tabs and windows were operated by invisible hands. He was in the field as the farmer sowed his seed and the birds swooped and pecked. And he was there to see him erect the scarecrow and to watch the corn grow so high he couldn't see over it. He lifted flaps in the earth to see wiggly worms and pulled a big cardboard wheel to tip the farmer's watering can. The last thing he saw was Scarecrow looking down from his support with a big smile. He waved and Scarecrow waved back, his sack-cloth face creasing with a friendly smile.

He woke up with pleasant memories and an infusion of childhood energy. And when Mr Kenneley said they were doing art in the afternoon he pulled on his painting pinny with enthusiasm. He painted a farmer in a field full of crops with Scarecrow dead centre and he was just about to lay his brush down and hang it up when he decided to add another scarecrow in. A boy sized one to keep Scarecrow company. Mr Kenneley said it was a great picture and when home time came around, he called his mummy over to tell her how hard he'd worked on it.

'I guess you liked that scarecrow book,' she said on the way home. 'How your mind works, I'll never know.' And when she got home, she put his painting on the fridge with Star Wars magnets.

In the evening he opened the scarecrow book and flicked to the page he dreamt about and sat cross-legged to stare into the scene. There were times he'd ask his mummy a question and she wouldn't answer, despite being right there in the room. And when he got up in her face to ask why she wasn't answering, she'd say she hadn't heard because she'd been lost in her book. He never understood what she meant by this, but he was lost in a similar way now. His attention anchored not by the words, but by the pop-up's beautiful illustrations.

And the more he stared the more real they seemed to become. Last year in Barcelona, he'd seen people dressed in strange costumes who kept themselves still as statues for ages and ages; making everyone laugh when they finally moved. Looking at these pop-ups was like looking at one of those statue people before you knew they were real. This was especially so with Scarecrow. He found it really hard to take his eyes from *him*. He seemed forever on the verge of moving and Ollie's expressionless vigilance stretched out for nearly an hour before his mother broke his trance.

'Okay story time,' she said. 'But I'm not reading that. You might like it, but I don't. Choose something else.'

Ollie returned the book to his desk, leaving it open at the page on which the scarecrow was all alone in the field. 'So he doesn't get lonely,' he said when his mummy frowned.

After a few minutes of messy browsing, he decided on what they now called *The Mole Book*. It was a story about a horse who lost his tail and not about moles at all. But there was a little mole in the background of every page who was forever up to mischief and his mummy had made up a story about her that was better than the real one. He hadn't heard the mole story for a long time and he clapped when she opened the first page.

But that night his dreams delivered him to the scarecrow book again. This time to the page where the scarecrow was looking into the little boy's room. Only *he* was the little boy and he was sitting up in bed looking at Scarecrow as he leaned through the open window. He could see past him to his abandoned support on a far-away hill: a crooked crucifix, aslant under a full moon. It was a scary sight but when Scarecrow spoke his voice was soothing, reminding Ollie of the friendly scarecrow from The Wizard of Oz, one of his mummy's favourite films.

'You wanna be my new friend?' Scarecrow asked.

'Where's the little boy?' he replied, looking around.

'Oh, don't worry about him. I want someone who can help me with the fields and pass the time telling stories about pirates who've lost their treasure and giant frogs with water pistols. And who knows – we might even find a funny little mole whose up to no good. So, what do you say? Will you be my friend Ollie? We'll be close as toes you and I. Like dock and nettle, buttercup and thistle.' Ollie looked past him to that crooked cross in the distant field, thinking it didn't look like fun. Scarecrow saw his concern and turned to wave a straw hand at the distant hillside, transforming it into a mid-summer pop-up scene with lots of cardboard sliders sticking out all ways and dozens of windows to open. 'You don't have to decide now young Ollie. Just think about it. We can play in the fields tonight and if you want to be my friend, all you have to do is write your name in my book. Come now - I'll give you a piggyback.'

The distant field now looked so much fun that Ollie ran to the window and climbed onto Scarecrow's back, whereupon he was whisked to the giant pop-up field. And there he spent the rest of his dreamtime. The sun was high and he skipped over the undulating shiny cardboard, following Scarecrows lead. They played hide and seek in corn rows, pulled tabs to reveal mice and chased them to distant burrows. Opened windows to reveal yucky worms and scared crows with sticks. It was more fun than he'd had in his entire life and he woke with a smile on his face.

Before school he remembered what the scarecrow said about writing his name in the book and he went to his desk and opened it on the first page. He took his favourite pen and wrote his name at the bottom of the list. He did in his bestest handwriting so as to impress Scarecrow – his tongue curling onto his top lip.

He went to school happy but at break time he couldn't keep up with his friends when they played tig. He was usually a top player, but when Billy tigged him, he stayed IT for the rest of the game. It wasn't that he got out of puff like some of his friends did, his arms and legs just got stiff, making it impossible to run fast. In the afternoon, his shoulders became stiff and he found himself lifting his arms up to stretch. When Mr Kennelley saw him do this, he stopped teaching, thinking he had a question. And when he persisted, he was sent out. Ollie had never been sent out before, but he didn't mind as it was such a relief to stretch without getting told off. At the end of the day, Mr Kenneley held him back to tell his mummy what he'd been up to.

'Why were you being silly in class?' she asked on the way home. 'It's not like you.'

'My arms were all stiff.'

'But why did you keep doing it? He said you were doing it over and over again.'

He shrugged and shook his head. But when a minute later he got stiff and stretched she stopped to remove his backpack, shaking her head as she tested the weight. 'It might be this. What have you got in here? A ton of bricks?'

'Just schoolbooks.'

'Well it's far too heavy for a boy your size. I'll talk to Mr Kenneley tomorrow and see if we can get you a locker or something.'

In the evening, he started to get stiff sitting down and could only relieve himself by standing up. When his mummy read his bedtime story, she noticed he was lying with his arms out to the sides.

'Still stiff?'

He nodded.

'Poor you,' she said, feeling his forehead for a temperature. 'If you're no better in the morning, I'll get you a doctor's appointment. See if they know what's going on.'

Ollie woke in the dead of night to find himself standing on his bed – arms out to his side and legs tight together. The pop-up book was open, but now it was huge and it overlapped the desk – its protruding scarecrow, life size, with its head almost touching the ceiling. His smile was gone and his face was all narrow and sucked in, like the scary double page pop-up that made his mummy gasp. It was so scary Ollie decided he didn't want to be Scarecrow's friend anymore. He tried to call for his mummy but the sound he made was not what he intended. His mouth felt all baggy and his voice was a crackle of dry straw.

His rigid body rose from the bed and floated across the room. He felt his toes brush the edge of the super-sized book before his feet came down on cold shiny paper. He was looking up at Scarecrow now, mirroring his cruciform posture.

'Are you ready to be my friend Ollie?' the nasty scarecrow asked from a mouth that was now a mouldering rip in a smelly old sack.

Ollie shook his head, trying desperately to communicate his change of heart with a voice that wouldn't work.

Scarecrow tipped his head, puckering his face. 'Oh, that's too bad. You wrote your name in my book and you can't take it back. That's the rule, didn't you know? And you did it in your bestest writing with your favourite pen... So, get ready Ollie, cause we're going in three... two... one.'

The book snapped shut and Ollie faceplanted into complete darkness...

Darkness endured – total and terrifying. He could hear his mother calling for him and Scarecrow sniggering close by. Somewhere above and behind him; folded flat against his back. He remembered the last pop-up in the book, of the mummy out searching for Little Tim and he started to cry. Or he thought he did, for he couldn't produce a single tear from his dry straw eyes.

Over time he felt swishing movements as the pop-up book was moved: tipped, rotated, laid flat and stood on end. And it could have been weeks, months or even years until he rose into the light again. But it wasn't into his bedroom as he had hoped, but a charity shop he didn't recognise. Above him was the face of a huge girl with pigtails and fairy dust cheeks. She was looking down with glassy fascination – her eyes moving between him and the scarecrow who was standing opposite and looking over with a smile Ollie knew was pretend.

'Can I get this one Mummy?' the girl said when a lady appeared above her.

'Yes honey – if that's what you want. Bring it to the till so we can pay.'

And with that the book began to close. The scenery tipped and blurred as he collapsed headfirst into the silky darkness beneath the grinning Scarecrow.

Memory Lane Bus Tours

Adam was strolling the baking pavement when he spotted an open-top bus, idling at the kerbside. He was no bus enthusiast, but it was a beautiful model – one of those old-fashioned types with an open back deck; its polished grab pole glinting in the sun. Its flank was illustrated with sepia photographs of bygone days at the seaside and the company's name was written above in a fancy black font: Memory Lane Bus Tours.

Standing confidently on the pavement with swarms of people breaking around him was the conductor; soliciting fares with a broad smile. Twin leather straps criss-crossed his white shirt: one supporting a money satchel, the other an archaic ticket machine.

'Hop aboard our open top and enjoy a picturesque trip to Scarborough's famous South Bay,' he said to the stream of tourists. 'Where soft sand and amusements await... Pound the fare and the wind in yer hair! ... Why walk on such a hot day, when you can go in comfort, learning a little local history from yours truly? Come on, footsore people of Scarborough... Pound the fare and the wind in yer hair!'

Adam made directly for him. It was August and sweltering and the few clouds that dared the blistering sky were unmoving – like painted things on blue canvas. He'd been planning to walk the Marine Drive, but he was besieged by heat and to sit with the wind in his hair was just what he needed.

The conductor greeted him with a game-show smile, his gleaming ticket machine almost too bright to look at. 'Ah good morning sir, just the one is it?'

Adam handed him a fiver and the conductor made change. But when he turned to board the bus, he called him back. 'Just a minute sir. You can't ride without a ticket.' He twisted a knob on the machine, which he now saw was embossed with an ornate letter B. The conductor's sleeves were rolled up to his elbows and his forearms were the hairiest ones Adam had ever seen. It occurred to him that such thick hair was likely to continue all over his body and that he must be suffering doubly in the heat. But he showed no sign – his skin dry and his shirt free of damp patches.

The machine whirred mechanically as the conductor turned the lever on the side of the machine – a pleasing sound that drew Adam's eyes, fastening them to an emerging ticket that seemed to take forever to be dispensed. It put him in mind of some video footage he'd seen that used high speed cameras to slow things down, enabling you to see bullets passing through melons or the intricate patterns raindrops made when hitting the surface of a lake. 'Have a good trip sir,' the conductor said, ripping the ticket off and breaking his trance. 'There's plenty of room up top.'

Adam pulled himself onto the bus using its shiny metal pole and with barely a glance at the lower deck, clomped up the spiral staircase. The lower deck was for people with arthritic knees, who abhorred drafts or were encumbered with pushchairs. Certainly not for young men with an image to uphold. He went right to the back, passing half a dozen passengers and flopping onto a seat with immaculate purple upholstery and polished chrome frame. He wondered if the bus ran to a timetable, as he didn't fancy the idea of baking under a hot sun while it filled up. But he quickly discovered he was happy to wait, looking over the edge and soaking up the sights: the armies of children heading for sandy trenches, rushing ahead of flustered, pack-horse parents; the ear-budded joggers and the selfish pavement cyclist weaving through them. He was above it all - there and not there. Looking down on them like a god.

It occurred to him he hadn't been on an open-top bus since he was seven years old. He remembered being fascinated by the way the seat frames vibrated with the purring engine and being compelled to rest his teeth upon the metal. Feeling them chatter with the vibration. It was the height of idiocy and his mother had been horrified, telling him his teeth would shatter if the bus suddenly pulled away. A warning that conjured a cartoon cat with its teeth falling out like broken glass, scaring him into never doing it again. He remembered that day with a smile and relaxed into his posh seat.

'Welcome everyone,' said an amplified voice when the bus was three-quarters full. It seemed to emanate from the middle of the deck, no doubt from speakers hidden under one of the seats. 'On our trip around the Marine Drive, I'll be taking you back through over a hundred years of history. We'll begin with the wall of white boards to your left, which currently hide a building site from which, the council have assured us, a new cinema complex will soon rise. The site was first developed in 1935 as the Motor Boat Pool where pairs of riders took circular trips in miniature motor boats. It opened as a swimming pool in 1938, extensively developed and renamed Waterscene in 1984 to become the largest water park in Europe.'

There was a pause and that pleasant whirring of the ticket machine filled the airwaves – a sound so exquisitely soothing that Adam melted into the upholstery. 'Now if you look through those boards and try really hard, you'll discover you can see back through time to its heyday... To the vast oval pool and its turbulent, glistening water... See the rising and sinking of begoggled heads, the scissoring of little legs, the thrash of arms and the streaks of orange arm bands... Encircling sunbeds with burnt bathers, abandoned towels and bottles of sunscreen... Hear the ratcheting turnstiles and the judder of the springboard, the thunderous plunge of bombers and belly-floppers and the delighted screams of wet children... Smell the chlorine, the Hawaiian Tropic and the trays of vinegar-soaked chips...'

As he spoke the boards became transparent and Adam found that he *could* see, hear and smell all the conductor asked him to. At first it was in the thin, low-definition images of his mind's eye. But the scene strengthened like an old polaroid, flooding with colour and sound that seemed to emanate from the hypnotic whine of the conductor's ticket machine. 'Feel the rough concrete under your feet and hear the blast of the lifeguard's whistle... See the huddle of expectant children staring up at a huge brimming bucket and watch it tip – covering them in a deluge of foaming water and knocking some from their feet.

'See the green tower looming above the pool and the twin blue slides spiralling down from either side... See the queue of shivering kids, jabbering excitedly as they make their slow, start-stop climb up flights of damp steps to where tanned lifeguards police the plunge with legs outstretched as barriers. Green deck shoes braced against blue fibreglass.

'Feel the excitement when a leg is lowered and the next child is nodded forward, to a dizzying view of the distant pool and into a torrent of cool water that rushes through her legs on its way to the first bend... Watch as she casts herself into that cold cascade, hips and shoulders battered as she rips around tight spirals, rising one side then the other, before being shot like a torpedo into a broth of white water.'

Adam saw this as if he was that child and it didn't strike him as strange. It was exhilarating and comforting in equal measure – his mind fully engrossed in a whirl of chlorinated fun. But then the bus pulled away and the waterpark faded, Adam's vision transitioning seamlessly back to reality – to the bustle of holidaymakers and the backdrop of heaving shops.

'On your left now is the Sands Development, a complex of shops and flats which recently replaced the Corner Café - a council venue comprised of a bar, restaurant and ballroom. Before that there was naught but Victorian bathing machines on this site. These *machines* were basically changing rooms on wheels. Carriages that were drawn into the water by horses, to where a bather could enter the sea in relative seclusion. The shyest clientele made use of modesty hoods or tilts as some called them – canvas awnings that could be let down to screen the user from other bathers. Same-sex dippers were employed to duck reluctant bathers in the incoming waves – with the medical bathing prescriptions standardised to three complete immersions.' He paused and that hypnotic whirring of his ticket machine begun again.

'See the man touting for business as he leads his horse along the beach. And see the young lady in her Sunday best, approaching with her purse... Watch as he helps her up the steps of a vacant bathing machine, yokes his horse to the seaward side and leads it into the sea... Hear the creak of the wooden wheels and the jangle of reigns... And smell the heaps of horseshit that stud the sand...

'Now take a look inside the bathing machine – at the row of hooks and hangers above a wooden bench bearing towels... See the fine lady struggle out of her expensive layers, frowning as she's jostled by the moving carriage. Not an ideal way to get changed, but time is money and the man out front has none to spare for kept women who spend more on petticoats than he earns in a year... See him untether his horse without delay and bring the back steps around to the front...

'See the fine lady appear in the seaward doorway, dressed in a flannel bathing suit. Hear the frothing waves breaking around the big wheels and take a hearty sniff of the salty air.' Adam sniffed and wasn't the least bit surprised when he smelt rock pools. A smell so redolent of childhood it deepened his relaxation. 'See yon dipper wading through the water to help: a ruddy-faced woman with broad shoulders, dressed in a flannel jacket topped with a straw hat... Watch the posh lady descend the steps, to be grabbed by the dipper when she attempts to withdraw from the coldness of the water. Like the horseman, the dipper has others waiting and no time for nonsense... Watch as she expertly draws the lady from her sheltered life and into the North Sea, her grip firm but not unkind. The muscles in the fine lady's neck roping as she clenches against the cold.

'See the dipper lay her back without warning and push her head beneath the waves... And see the fine lady fight for her feet with flailing arms, to surface with a string of gasps. Styled hair now flat to her head. But don't miss the dipper's smirk. She enjoys this part of the job - the exhilarating reversal of power as she dunks her supposed betters. See her dip the shivering lady a second and third time before helping her back up the steps...

'On we go now folks... As we turn onto the Marine Drive, I want you to look out across the bay...'

As he spoke Adam lost consciousness, eyes suddenly vacant and face twitching – his gaze trained out to sea, but no longer seeing. It lasted no more than twenty seconds, but when he came to, he was dribbling down his chin. He knew right away what had happened, because it had happened several times before. He'd had a seizure – the latest of a string his epilepsy specialist was trying to tame. He wiped the spittle away his forearm, feeling more than a little self-conscious as he looked around. It was the first time he'd looked around since the conductor started talking and he saw that everyone was looking out to sea, seemingly spellbound by some distant happening. Their faces were blank in the extreme and not a single person was stirred by his sweeping gaze. By far, the creepiest thing he'd ever seen. The passengers were quiet and still, the sun burning their faces and the breeze tossing their hair – the focus of their collective stare, some invisible sinkhole that seemed to be draining their souls. He looked out with them, but saw nothing to explain their eerie fascination.

He heard the conductor's boots on the stairs and he soon appeared on the top deck, talking into a little mic that was pinned to his collar. 'If you turn to the cliffs now, you'll be looking at the former site of The Queen's Parade Tramway.' All heads turned in unison and now *this* was the creepiest thing Adam had ever seen. 'It's the least well known of Scarborough's five cliff lifts, only two of which survive today. Extant from 1878-1887 – it worked on a water balance principle, using a 3.5 horsepower engine to pump water from a tank under the station.'

The conductor leant over an elderly couple as he talked – reaching into the man's pocket and removing his wallet. He tipped the contents into his satchel and replaced it. Adam couldn't see the old man's face, but he didn't seem to mind and had even lifted his hip to aid the extraction. 'Its twin cars lifted and lowered passengers 218 feet over an average gradient of 1 in 2.3,' the conductor went on, 'passing through a tunnel just above the lower station.' He was reaching over the man to the old lady now and appeared to be riffling through her bag. Adam felt the need to intervene, but a profound lethargy had taken resident in his bones, anchoring him to his seat. The conductor had the passengers under some sort of spell, Adam realised. His seizure had short circuited it, but he wasn't entirely free of its influence. 'The tram proved to be a financial disaster and after a landslide in 1887, never reopened. No trace of it remains and you'll be hard pressed to find one of the few remaining photographs.'

When the conductor looked along the bus for his next victim, he saw Adam staring at him – the only face that wasn't directed to the cliff. There was a flash of anger in his eyes and he stomped over, pulling on seat backs. And he was flickering now – his body replaced every few seconds by a green hologram. An image too brief to fully appreciate.

'Interesting,' the conductor said with his microphone switched off. 'A little more crank's all you need young man. Now be a good fellow and look at the machine.' He whirred the lever several times and Adam's thoughts spiralled into mush with the sight of the emerging ticket. When it was done, the conductor ripped it off and threw it away. Then he gripped Adam's jaw and took a long look into his eyes.

'That's better. Now if you'll look out to sea, we'll get on with the tour.' Adam did as asked, the crimes he had witnessed suddenly vague and unimportant.

'On the left is where North Bay Promenade Pier once projected into what, until World War One was called the German Sea. Opened in 1869, it was 1000 feet long and 23 feet wide, terminating in a pier head shelter. Its length supported on cast iron piles joined by wrought iron girders. Ornate seating ran the length of both sides, curving into six pairs of opposed recesses that increased the width of the pier to 35 feet. In 1889 it passed to new owners who enlarged the pier head and added an entrance pavilion, containing shops, a restaurant and concert rooms.' Another pause, followed by more metallic whirring.

'Look with me now, vile people of Scarborough... See the entrance with its high turrets and archway - the shops on either side with their latticed windows and gathered three quarter nets. Step past the flat-capped attendant to where children stand around penny arcades... where kiosks sell penny licks and ball bearings rattle through mahogany encased mazes... Hear the clink of porcelain from the tea shop and the clomp of shoes against hardwood boards...

'Now skip down the steps onto the sunny pier and wind your way through crowds... See the ladies in white flounced skirts and blouses; straw hats decorated with flowers and colourful ribbons. Some bearing brushed-chiffon parasols which rest on their shoulders, lace-gloved hands twisting their ivory handles... See the men in their three-piece lounge suits and flat caps. Others in morning jackets and bowlers... And see the old ladies in black bonnets, pulling at their shawls and frowning at racing children... Look at the man over here, raising his eyes from his fluttering newspaper to call to a barrowman selling whelks. And the boy over there, crinkling his face as he looks through a mounted telescope... See Tom Carrick's troupe of seaside Pierrots performing on the pier head in their loose white blouses and pantaloons, powdered faces and conical hats. Large black buttons and frilled collarets. Beyond them all, see the diver somersaulting off a high platform to rapturous applause.'

Adam saw what was asked of him but not in the way the conductor wanted. Like the others he was helplessly immersed in his magically generated vignette, but his seizure had made him aware of his predicament and he was able to focus outside the boundary of the conductor's narrow instructions. His eyes were drawn to a man in a bowler hat, his starched collar almost hidden by a monstrous beard. An Albert Watch guard looped down from his waistcoat and he wore a signet ring on his left little finger, engraved with the letter B. It was the conductor – the very same man who was currently reaching into a young lady's pocket across the aisle. This Victorian version of him was entertaining a lady with a flower hat and fox stole. He couldn't hear what he was saying, but the lady was blushing, laughing and pushing his shoulder, embarrassed no doubt by some crude flattery. Boisterous children were playing close by, bumping her with regularity. As she chatted, one produced a knife and cut her purse, freeing the contents into a little bag.

There was a sudden change in Adam's viewpoint and now he was on the sands, watching the conductor strolling between the iron supports where the same children were gathered. The boy who cut the lady's purse separated from the others and handed him the bag. The conductor patted his head, tucked the bag into the folds of his jacket and strolled away.

'On 7th January 1905,' the conductor went on, 'a severe storm destroyed the whole structure, isolating the pavilion on the pier head. Part of the blame was directed toward the designer who was said to have built the pier too low, not accounting for the heights of spring tides and storm swell.' Adam saw the isolated pier head, like a monstrous jelly fish, risen from hostile seas. And he saw the conductor swigging a bottle of whiskey in the dilapidated salon and laughing maniacally as the waves crashed through the twisted wreckage. 'The ruined pier was sold for scrap, but the owner wasn't willing to give up the pavilion as he didn't want to lose the liquor licence attached to it

– soon mooting a cable car system to keep it in use.' There was a ripple of laughter from the entranced passengers. 'This of course never came to fruition and the pavilion disappeared a few months later... When the tide is low you can still see the remains of the foundations sticking out of the sand... The rotten teeth of a bygone age.'

'Moving on, spoilt citizens of the twenty-first century. If you cast your eyes up the cliff to a point between the castle and the first hotels – you'll be looking at the spot where between 1898 and 1907 a 100-foot rotating observation tower once stood. Named Warwick's Tower after the man who designed it. It was widely deemed to be a blemish on this beautiful coastline and was demolished in 1907. Look it up on your beloved phones if you don't believe me, cos nothing's real unless it's on the internet now, is it? You despicable spoon-fed zombies.'

The conductor proceeded to immerse the passengers in a favoured vision of the landmark, but once again Adam saw through it to a deeper one. The conductor was there again – now in a top hat, paisley cravat and gleaming tie pin. A black cape embroidered with a gold letter B hung from his broad shoulders. His chin was shaved and his face furnished with an enormous curled moustache and mutton chops.

Adam watched the conductor approach the tower's ticket office through thick fog. He jumped the turnstile, grabbing a man who was cashing up and manhandling him onto the platform... The scene changed to one at a distance: the platform rotating and climbing ever higher, the whining and clanging of metal covering the man's pleas for mercy as the conductor griped his collar with a hairy fist, pinning him to the guard rails... Another change of scene and the platform was fully raised, the conductor holding the man over the edge by his ankle, his desperate promises to pay a bigger share of his takings, punctuated by fearful cries that knife across the fog-clogged bay.

The image blurred out of focus as the bus trundled on, replaced by the reality of the castle cliff.

'Work on the Marine Drive began in 1897. Although the drive was completed in 1904, damage caused by the same storm that wrecked the pier, delayed its opening until 1908. Ten years ten months and ten days it took to complete – back breaking work I doubt you undeserving sluggards can even imagine... See the steam powered cranes running along rickety wooden gantries - watch as they lower blocks to labouring men who fix them in place against an incoming tide. Dangerous work, for laughable remuneration.' This Adam saw with the rest of them. No deeper vision here.

'If you look to the left, you'll see Hairy Bob's Skate Park and if we're lucky the kids might treat us to a few stunts. In the background, part hidden in the high grass you can see Hairy Bob's Cave after which the park is named. As you can see, it's not really a cave, rather a boulder with a door and two windows chiselled in – the doorway just big enough for a child to sit inside. There are many rumours about the origin of the cave, the most pervasive that it was cut by one of the men who worked on the drive.

The conductor began to paint another picture and the passengers smiled, seeing a man in overalls chipping out flakes of stone, a masonry hammer and chisel in his hand and the sun glistening off his sweaty back. But Adam was seeing deeper again – to a truth hidden from everyone else. He saw the boulder falling from the weathered cliff as a bunch of workers toiled beneath the gantry – a ray of tumbling green light emanating from its centre. A worker straightened as it fell, the only one of the gang to see it. It was the conductor again – this time dressed in grubby overalls. And he was instantly transfixed by the light. A light generated by a lifeforce that had been trapped in the castle headland for hundreds of years. The dust had barely settled around the boulder when this version of the conductor took his tools and ran up the cliff; his fellow workers shouting after him. 'Hey Bob! What yer doing? The gaffer'll blow his top if he catches you.' But he wasn't listening. He reached the boulder and attacked it with hammer and chisel, eyes staring ferociously through the rock to an inner radiance which only he could see.

There was a jump in time and the gaffer was climbing after him, soon firing him when he continued hammering after several demands for him to return to work. 'Bob's gone mad,' he told the baffled work crew as he clambered back down.

In quick time Adam saw the day go by, the workers going home and the day turning dark – all the while Bob hammering away without a break. And as the moon rose above the castle walls, he finally broke through to the inner radiance that so bewitched him – an ancient life force that instantly flowed into him. He staggered away and dropped his tools, now flickering between a sickly green hologram and his true form. He fell between rocks, thrashing and roaring on his hands and knees. But his struggle soon abated and he became still. Hours later he stood and looked around, straighter than before and with a wily intelligence behind his eyes. Once Hairy Bob to his co-workers, now something more - a Victorian demon who would become the scourge of the North Bay. A hustler, racketeer and thieving bus conductor.

Adam came back to reality and the legend that was Hairy Bob was still filching from the pockets of spellbound tourists. He had a rush of clarity and understood his predicament with absolute certainty. The conductor had woven his immersive scenes with ancient magic, using memories of his old stomping grounds, places in which he had stolen and intimidated his way to riches. And Adam knew that if his seizure had occurred when he first sat down on the bus, he would have seen him in those earlier scenes too – perhaps breaking into lockers at the pool and pilfering purses in bathing machines.

The conductor caught him staring again and stormed over. 'You've seen a lot more than you should,' he said, jabbing a finger against Adam's forehead. His image was flickering quicker now and Adam realised the hologram inside was the real Bob and that his outer flesh was nothing more than a respectable disguise. Bizarrely, his hologram was hairier still - hair sprouting from his shirt and flowing from his forearms like horse manes. Bristling sideburns linked by a monobrow jungle. And his expression was truly maniacal. The whites of his eyes were cracked marble around green glass irises that looked like they had been crushed under a boot heel. It was a face that belonged in an asylum, pressed to the bars of a padded cell.

'Hairy Bob!' said Adam.

'I've never liked that name and there was a time when I'd open a man's throat for using it. But I wouldn't want your fancy blood ruining my new upholstery.' His jaw clenched and his nostrils flared. 'Now look at the machine and know your life depends on you tuning in. Cos you ain't getting off this bus with that nonsense in your head.'

He began winding his machine and his flickering subsided, his eyes becoming soft and disarming, his snarl morphing into a compassionate smile. 'Better?' he asked, gripping Adam's shoulder in a grandfatherly way.

'Yeah. Better now,' he replied, though he wasn't sure what he was claiming to be better from.

'*Bob the Builder,*' the conductor sung as he walked away, looking over his shoulder. '*Can he fix it?*'

'*Bob the Builder – yes he can,*' Adam sang, as if it were the most normal thing in the world.

'Very good,' the conductor said, slapping a dreamy passenger on the back. 'Old Bob's got a full house.'

He fiddled with his mic and his voice was blasting from the speakers again. 'When the Marine Drive first opened the toll of one penny was levied on walkers, horseback and motorcycle riders, and those travelling in a carriage or motor car. And if you look ahead you can see the tollhouse – now occupied by Her Majesty's Coastguard.'

This time there was no magical vignette and the passengers heard only his words. The bus navigated the roundabout onto Sandside, passing Luna Park's Ferris wheel and a harbour of jostling boats. The water was high and calm; black and mirror-like. If there was a Scarborough anthem, it was that which now filled Adam's ears: the layered cacophony of seagulls, the ping and bleeps of arcades and the revving of engines. And if there was a Scarborough aroma it was that which filled his nose – fish and chips, doughnuts and fried onions, tinged with swirling exhaust fumes.

'We'll be pulling up shortly,' the conductor said. 'Thank you for riding Memory Lane Bus Tours. Our service runs from ten till six every Sunday and if you've enjoyed yourself, please tell your friends. And remember, pound the fare and the wind in yer hair.'

The bus drew up by the harbour slipway. Adam was the last passenger off the top deck and as he reached the stairs the conductor stepped up, barring his way with a broad grin. 'Nice spell of weather we're having.'

'Sure is.'

'Did you enjoy the ride?'

'Yeah, it was pretty good.'

'Any suggestions on how we can improve?' The conductor smiled expectantly, looking genuinely interested in what he might have to say. His hand on the lever of his machine, as if ready to dispense a ticket. But Adam couldn't think of anything constructive. If truth be told, he'd dozed off in the middle of the ride and could only remember the beginning and the end.

'Can't think of anything. It was great... Just keep doing what you're doing I suppose.'

It sounded lame to his ears, but the conductor seemed pleased and stepped out of his way. 'Many thanks sir and have a nice day.'

Adam stepped onto a sun-bleached pavement and the bus rumbled away, puffing black fumes from its exhaust. He didn't see the conductor watching him from the top deck, eyes narrowed and face set in a contemplative mask.

He saw a boy licking ice-cream from a huge cone and decided it was just what he needed. He crossed the road and joined the queue outside the Harbour Bar, scrutinising the sales board as he shuffled forward. Settling on a lemon twist the very second an aproned girl leant forward to take his order. He pulled his wallet out, discovering a bare notes compartment as she handed him the cone. 'Hang on,' he said, feeling through his pockets in rising panic. 'I can't find my money.'

The serving girl frowned sceptically. 'Step aside then, while I serve this lady,' she said, taking the cone back. 'I'll put it in the rack while you look.'

Adam moved to one side, feeling several pairs of eyes on him as he riffled through his pockets. Some shook their heads. When he tried to remember what was in his wallet when he paid for the bus ticket, there was a metallic whining in his head and he remembered that he'd bought it with the last of his money. He looked at his ice cream which was already dribbling down the cone, shaking his head apologetically when the serving girl glanced in his direction. He turned away, stepping out from the shade of the parlour's wide awning and into the heat of the day.

THE END

Also by J.B.Forsyth

Twisted:Volume One

Twisted:Volume:Two

Twisted:Volume Three

Twisted:Volume Four

Absence: Whispers and Shadow

Absence: Mist and Shadow

Tales of the Westland: Volume One

Tales of the Westland: Volume Two

Printed in Great Britain
by Amazon